SWEPT AWAY

Cay David

A KISMET™ Romance

METEOR PUBLISHING CORPORATION
Bensalem, Pennsylvania

For all the rainy days she kept me entertained, for all the imaginary hurts she healed, and for all the countless times she listened, this book is dedicated to the memory of my grandmother, Pearl Moore.

To my husband, Pieter, my constant source of support and love. Have I told you lately you're the most important thing in my life?

CAY DAVID

Cay David is a native Texan whose idea of Heaven is a day on the beach with her singularly handsome husband beside her, a good, thick book in her lap, and a cool, tall drink in her hand. Most days, however, she can be found at her computer, working on her next book, or at her desk, tracking down exotic gems for clients of her jewelry design firm. **SWEPT AWAY,** her second Meteor release, reflects her love of the white sands of Florida and all its romantic possibilities.

Other books by Cay David:

ONE

"Where is he?"

"How the hell would I know?" The old woman looked suspiciously at her from behind the barely open door. "Am I his keeper or something?"

With one hand stretched across her forehead, Charlotte Huntington tried to shield her eyes from the blinding Florida sunlight. She failed, but her gaze didn't waver from the wrinkled face staring back at her.

Her patience intact, she started over. "I left several messages on his machine, in addition to my letters, but Mr. Gibson never replied. I flew in here from Denver just to—"

"You coulda flew in on your own broom, honey, and Sam still wouldn't get up before noon to meet ya." The old lady opened the door a little wider and leaned against the frame, her cigarette smoke billowing out as she stared at Charlotte's black suit and single strand of perfect pearls. When her watery blue eyes returned to Charlotte's face, a flash of sympathy came, then went. "Ain't you kinda hot in all them clothes?"

Charlotte's fingers went to the dark bangs now falling across her forehead. She tried to push them into place, but the humidity pulled them back down. Actually, she was about to die. She'd left Colorado mountains quietly blanketed with the last snows of the season. There was white here, too, but it was sand, and it was baking.

Ignoring her discomfort and the woman's question, Charlotte licked lips that had last seen lipstick ten hours ago and tried not to cough as the cloud of acrid smoke hit her. "C . . . can you simply tell me where I might find Mr. Gibson?"

Under her faded red swimsuit, the old woman shrugged her shoulders, her leathery skin wrinkling even more. "Ya might try down on the beach—that's where he usually sleeps it off."

Sleeps it off? Charlotte jumped back as the woman slammed the door, the conversation obviously finished.

Almost as finished as I am, Charlotte thought, turning back to face the steamy parking lot, *if I don't take care of this. And what the hell does "sleep it off" mean?* That doesn't sound good. The weight of her leather briefcase pulled at her arms, and a trickle of moisture inched down between her shoulder blades.

There was nothing left to do but traipse down to the beach. She turned and headed for the side of the building.

As she walked past the twelve units of Safe Harbor, Charlotte shook her head in disgust. Tall weeds grew with careless abandon in the flower beds, and the short brick walls that separated each unit's patio from the next were crumbling at the corners. Splotched paint covered the weathered wooden exteriors, and, from what she'd seen of the older woman's unit, things were not much better inside. Above Charlotte's head, whipping back and forth in the strong breeze, was the only thing that looked well cared for—a bright American flag.

Continuing down the wooden boardwalk, Charlotte stared at the flag, its perfection a puzzling contrast to the rundown condos. Suddenly, she pitched forward, her heel trapped in one of the cracked boards.

Windmilling her arms and cursing loudly, she dropped her briefcase and managed to catch her balance before falling down completely. Bending over to untangle her foot, she looked around self-consciously. Screaming oaths in broad daylight was not something Charlotte Huntington normally did. As she finally freed the two-hundred dollar shoe and held it up for inspection, another curse, however, escaped. From top to bottom, the leather heel was ripped open, the white plastic underneath gleaming like a broken bone.

With a snort of disgust, she crammed the mutilated shoe back on her foot, picked up her briefcase—also sporting a new scratch from an exposed nail—and continued, madder than ever. If Sam Gibson had been doing his job, she wouldn't even be here, sweating like a pig and feeling like an idiot.

Rounding the corner, Charlotte's eyes automatically squinted against the glare. White sand—sand so fine and bleached it looked like sugar—stretched before her, curving into dunes topped with tall swaying grass. She shaded her eyes once again, but saw nothing. With a grim frown of determination, she stepped off the boards and into the powder, scanning the beach on either side.

Finally, she spotted what looked like the tip of an umbrella hiding behind a dune down on her right. Tightening her grip on her briefcase and ignoring the sand filling her shoes, she headed in that direction.

What kind of man would be lying on a beach at three o'clock on a Monday afternoon? Any decent human being would be working for a living. And in Sam Gibson's case that work included taking care of Safe Harbor. Hah! What

a misnomer. "Safe" it definitely wasn't. Why she'd practically broken her neck on the boardwalk. They could be
sued for something like that—how could he let such a
potentially dangerous situation go without attention?

Her calves ached as she reached the crest of the dune,
but Charlotte ignored the pain and plowed ahead, her con-
viction growing that Sam Gibson was nothing but trouble.
When she stopped and stared at the man stretched out
asleep under the gaudy umbrella ten feet ahead of her, she
knew she was right.

He lay perfectly still, his eyes closed, obviously deeply
asleep—or passed out. She wanted to shake him into
wakefulness, but rousing him from his stupor also meant
disturbing the scruffy dog beside him, and Charlotte hesitated. Trying to decide what to do, she studied Sam
through slitted eyes.

Heedless of her stare, he sprawled gracefully across a
towel that was much too short for his long body. Tanned
legs extended into powdery sand while his head rested on
an incongruous bed pillow. On his right side, the dog
shared the shade of the brightly colored umbrella, his long
snout stretched across Sam's flat stomach. Four empty
beer cans, turned upside down and halfway buried,
guarded his left flank.

Charlotte had thought the situation couldn't get any
worse when she'd pulled into the bumpy parking lot of
the Safe Harbor condominium project and seen its condition, but now something told her she'd been wrong.

Terribly wrong.

Her unwillingness to surrender to her temper checked
her desire to revive the sleeping man. She took two deep,
calming breaths and stared at the dog. He looked as dere-
lict as his master. The elongated, canine body hinted at a
dachshund-like heritage, but any other resemblance to such
a lofty parentage ended there. His dirty-blond coat was

coarse and irregular, as if a blind man had trimmed it. As Charlotte shifted in the sand, he opened one eye and swiveled his short, tufted ears toward her, growling softly.

Her eyes strayed back to Sam, the sun scorching her neck. She knew this entire mess really had nothing to do with him, but her anger continued to blossom. Never impulsive, she stood quietly and thought about her next move while staring at Sam's relaxed body—his relaxed, *almost naked* body, she realized with a start.

Unconsciously, she licked her lips as she stared at his. He had the kind of mouth, full and lush, that made you think about things you shouldn't—dark rooms and low music and hot hands against bare skin. As she watched, he smiled slightly in his sleep, and two deep lines connected the outer corners of his nose with the edges of his mouth.

She pulled her eyes from his lips, but that got her into even more trouble. Fine, darkish-blond hair, dusted with gray, decorated his chest, starting from a wide triangle between two brown nipples and spreading to a point that disappeared below his navel. The curls looked as if they would feel soft beneath her fingers—*very* soft and *very* sexy.

Nervously, she ran her thumb over the shank of the small diamond ring on her left hand. The last bare-chested man she'd seen—Jonathan, her boss and fiancé—came into her mind. There was definitely no comparison between the two.

Judging from the skimpy, faded bathing suit this man wore low on his slim hips, there were a few other comparisons where Jonathan might come up short. Charlotte blushed immediately but couldn't rein in her thoughts or stop her eyes from lingering on that very specific bulge.

"Well, Miss Huntington, see something you like?"

Charlotte sprang back in surprise, horrified at being

caught, but even angrier that he'd been watching her watching him. "How in the hell did you know who I was?" she blurted out.

He slowly raised his eyebrows and opened his eyes wider. Charlotte was instantly seduced.

They were electric blue—a shade that was more than appealing, more than gorgeous, more than unexpected. Like double magnets, they reached inside of her and pulled out an automatic response from deep within the pit of her stomach—a response that left her trembling and thoroughly shocked.

He smiled, deep wrinkles creasing the skin beside those incredible eyes, then stretched his arms out above his head before finally answering. "I got your messages. No one else is looking for me—that I know of. As the song goes, 'IT HAD TO BE YOU.' " Yawning widely, he pulled his arms back down and slipped his hands under his head.

On their own volition, her eyes traveled to the underside of his upper arms where hardened muscles pushed the veins close to the surface of his skin. She could see the blood coursing through his body. This new position also widened his chest, slimmed his already narrow hips, and made Charlotte swallow hard.

"Besides," he continued, "you look like a Charlotte Huntington. Neat, expensive . . ." His startling blue stare went up and down her suit, lingering at particular spots before moving on slowly. "Uptight."

She pursed her lips, her fingers going nervously to the high neck of her blouse. The long-sleeved suit that had been perfect for a cloudy summer day in Denver was beginning to feel like a designer straightjacket. Disregarding the dots of moisture forming above her upper lip, Sam Gibson's innuendos, and her unexpected reaction to him, she spoke primly. "I had to knock on doors until I found someone at the property who could tell me where you were." She paused with what she hoped was a disapproving look. "Mr. Gibson, if you knew I was coming, why didn't you wait for me in your office? It would have made things a little easier for me, you know."

He sat up slowly and held out one hand toward the emerald water, curling into waves twenty feet away. "This *is* my office, sweetheart." Patting the towel beside him, he looked back at her. "This is my desk, and this—" he indicated the sleepy-eyed dog beside him, "is Punch, my faithful assistant. He doesn't complain when I come in late, he's the most loyal employee I've ever had, and his wages are extremely low—an occasional loving word and two bowls of Dog Chow a day."

Despite the heat and her anger, Charlotte's mouth twitched with amusement. The dog sounded like a better employee than some of her coworkers.

Sam's lips pulled up in a high-wattage acknowledgment of her tentative smile. "Why don't you just take off that coat of yours and sit down? I've got a few cold ones left in the cooler. We'll pop one or two, and you can tell me what's got you so hot under the collar." As if to prove his point, he leaned over and reached inside a Styrofoam ice chest.

Growing hotter by the second, she stared at the ice-cold beer in his outstretched hand, but shook her head, feeling as if she were moving in slow motion. Like a broken string of pearls, one bead of perspiration rolled between her breasts, another down her back. She wouldn't last much longer in this heat, and her temporary amusement over the dog fled. "No, thank you, Mr. Gibson. I never drink beer."

"Well, I do, so I'm sure you won't mind if I have one. Right?"

"Mr. Gibson—"

"Sam, please, Charlotte. No one has ever called me

'Mr. Gibson.' A few other things maybe, but never 'Mr.' ''

Black dots began to swim before Charlotte's eyes, and a jackhammer headache sounded behind them. She dropped her eyelids against the sight of the half-naked man, the glaring sun, and the dog who had now moved closer to her and was licking her ankles with great relish.

Opening her eyes, she took a deep breath and swept back her bangs, trying unobtrusively to push at the dog with her foot. He lifted his upper lip, growled, then abandoned her ankles for her calves, sliding his slobbery nose up and down her leg to leave a wet, slimy trail.

Charlotte gritted her teeth and tried to ignore the animal, wishing she could do the same for her rising temperature. Tilting her head toward the condominium project behind them, she spoke. "Mr. Gibson, I am shocked at the condition of Safe Harbor. I was aware the units needed *some* work, but . . .''

He leaned his head back and took a long draw from the beer. She watched the column of his neck move as he swallowed, then spoke. "Yeah, I guess they could stand a coat of paint."

She looked down at him and fought the wave of dizziness threatening her. "Paint?" she said, her voice rising another octave. "Paint? They're falling down, damnit to hell.''

He raised his eyebrows. "Why, Charlotte, you shock me. I can't believe an obviously well-bred, well-educated woman like yourself would use such language—''

She blushed involuntarily, hating the heat suffusing her face and hating even more her slip-up. She *shouldn't* be talking like that, but she was so hot she was about to pass out. Her voice turned almost desperate, and despite her best intentions, she swayed involuntarily. "Can we please go somewhere cooler and discuss this?''

Some vestige of manners must have risen to the front of his consciousness, and with a quickness that surprised her, he rose and took the leather case from her hand. "Of course. Let's go to my unit. I have some iced tea in the refrigerator. That's probably more your speed."

The three of them trudged silently back to the units, Charlotte so hot she could hear the blood rushing in her ears. She wanted to stop but wouldn't, and the black dots behind her eyes were multiplying. She didn't know what bothered her most; the heat, the humidity, or the smell of suntan lotion and beer that wafted to her from Sam's copper-colored skin as he lead her down the beach.

They finally reached the condo at the end of the complex, and Sam held the door open to a wide, screened-in porch. As Charlotte stepped forward, the dog jumped ahead of her, and suddenly her feet and the dog's tangled. Already unsteady, she swayed against the man behind her. Dropping the briefcase and the cooler, he caught her weight against his broad chest then grabbed both of her arms.

Through a growing haze, she felt the warmth of his embrace, and she looked down at the dark fingers holding her forearms. Several grains of sand had fallen from his hands to her jacket. She noticed how starkly the white contrasted with the black. Then, she passed out.

With a grunt of surprise, Sam caught Charlotte's limp body before it could slide completely to the floor. "Aw, sh—" he muttered under his breath. Struggling to handle her dead weight, he finally managed to get one hand under her knees and the other around her shoulders. He picked her up, and her head lolled against his shoulder like a baby's. She seemed to weigh less than Punch, who now stood at his feet, grinning from ear to ear, trying to look innocent of any involvement.

Her suit scratched against his bare skin, and Sam wondered again about a person who would wear a long-sleeved jacket to Florida. Shaking his head, he carried her to the rattan couch at one end of the porch and deposited her on the cushions, putting her down less gracefully than she probably would have demanded had she been awake.

He'd made it a personal policy several years ago, after an incident in Singapore, not to undress women who were unconscious, but this was clearly an emergency. He slipped off her jacket then unbuttoned all but one of the buttons on her blouse, determined to let the breeze of the overhead fan cool her heat-flushed skin. As the silky fabric parted, Sam drew in his breath with an eloquent whistle. He would have sworn that Charlotte Huntington was the type of woman who would wear white cotton underwear—the kind he used to see hanging on the line out behind Aunt Hattie's farmhouse. Nothing like the lacy half-bra that teased his eyes now.

With a quick glance to her still face, he gave in and allowed his gaze to greedily run over the swells of her breasts. Dark-rose nipples teased the edge of the revealing bra, almost daring Sam to keep his hands to himself. The satiny skin looked warm and soft, but he knew better than to touch. She might wear underwear from Frederick's of Hollywood, but she looked like trouble—the kind he didn't want.

Charlotte Huntington was clearly a woman who would make life miserable. She'd organize your sock drawer, make you wear underwear, tell you to clean out the garage. He stared at her and ran one hand over the stubble on his face.

Her manner didn't match her body anymore than her underwear matched her personality. And for just a second, Sam wondered how she'd look with her hair down and her interest up. He shook his head. It didn't matter; she wasn't his type at all, too prim, too proper, even if the bra did raise his—eyebrows.

Reluctantly, he walked back to the door and picked up the cooler and her briefcase, setting them both near the couch. Padding into the house, he returned a second later with iced tea and a cool towel. Standing beside the couch, Sam couldn't seem to get his eyes away from her.

Her hair was the kind you'd like to lose yourself in, he thought idly, but she fixed it like an old lady—twisted up in a bun behind her head. Dark, thick bangs hung down across her forehead and on each side, escaping tendrils stuck to her neck as if they'd been pasted there. The flush of heat still darkened her face and chest, but underneath the redness, her skin appeared fine and pale. In fact, he could even see the faint blue veins that ran across the tops of her breasts.

He set the tray down on the coffee table, then reached to the other end of the couch and slipped off her shoes. Sam didn't have much experience in examining women's footwear, but he knew enough to recognize how expensive this pair must have been. The black leather was soft and supple, and the name stamped inside had a definite Italian ring to it. The long tear on the heel told him she must have found that broken board on the wooden sidewalk out front. Balancing the delicate shoe in his hand then dropping it with a thud, he shook his head. He'd better fix that damn board, he thought for the umpteenth time.

Sam turned back to look at the outstretched woman. She hadn't moved an inch, but he knew she was still alive. Moving closer, he could just barely see her pulse throbbing rapidly in the hollow at the base of her throat. Strangely, the sight elevated his own heart rate.

Her eyes were still closed, her face only slightly less red than when they'd first arrived. He draped the cold towel over her forehead. And perfume, a heady mixture of flowers and spice entirely too sensual for the pale-skinned woman, rose to tease his nose. He groaned deep in his throat, then cut off the sound and stood abruptly. It'd been too damned long, he thought, if a woman like Charlotte Huntington could turn him on.

He reached over to lift the cold towel from her forehead, then gently sponged her face. A few minutes later, her eyes fluttered open and she raised her hand. "W . . . what . . . wh . . . where am I? What happened?"

"You passed out," he answered. "You're on my back porch."

As if a ten-pound weight anchored her wrist, she slowly raised her arm to take the cloth from his hand. "H . . . here, I can do that."

He relinquished the cloth. "How do you feel?"

"Like hell." Her face flushed darker. "I can't believe I did something so stupid." She looked down at her prone body, the cold towel clutched in her hand. "W . . . what happened to my clothes? My jacket?"

Watching Charlotte grab the edges of her parted blouse, Sam sat back down on the edge of the sofa, the springs protesting at his weight. "I was trying to help," he said mildly, picking up the glass of iced tea then swiveling back to face her. She looked like she'd just swallowed a lemon. "But don't worry." He dropped his voice. "I'll never tell a soul you wear lace on your bras."

Her entire body went still as she sucked in her breath. Then she spoke, her voice icy with disdain. "Thank you *so-o* much, Mr. Gibson. I'd really appreciate that discretion."

"Anytime. I'd be happy to do more . . ."

She closed her eyes again, and much to his surprise, she didn't even react to his words as she replaced the towel on her forehead. Obviously, she still felt bad.

He turned to fish out an ice cube from the glass of tea

then twisted back toward her. His hand pressed the ice against the pulse point at the base of her neck and held it there.

Immediately, her fingers shot out and grabbed his wrist, but there was no strength in her grip. "What do you think you're doing?"

"Cooling you off."

"That's not necessary," she insisted. "I'm fine."

Even as she spoke, however, her eyes fluttered down, and she sighed gently. She let her hands slip back to the cushions, and the blouse parted once more.

As though she were in a carnival funhouse that distorted her perceptions instead of her appearance, Charlotte's internal world tilted. A riot of sensations combined and ran together—the chill of the ice against her skin, the rough hand that held it there, the quiet swish of the fan, the lingering smell of salt air.

Sam lifted his icy fingers from her throat, and a cold river of water trickled deliciously between her breasts. She twisted her head against the pillow on the sofa and listened to the surf outside. The fan continued to whirl above her head, and Charlotte marveled that she was allowing this man—a complete stranger—to take care of her like this.

His hands took the cloth from her face. They were broad hands, capable hands, hands that would be comfortable working on a car, holding a baby, doing anything they wanted to. From a glass on the table, he poured ice water on the towel then returned it to her forehead. The exquisite coldness eased the last of the heat away as she closed her eyes once more. Fingers, still warm from the sun, glided to the side of her face to smooth the hair back.

He stuck a straw between her lips. "Sip slowly. It's only iced tea, but the caffeine will help."

The cold liquid filled her mouth then slipped down her throat like a toboggan on a snowy mountain. Never had iced tea tasted so good before. He removed the straw before she was ready, but when her eyes flickered open in protest, he shook his head. "Not too much at first. You'll get sicker than you already are."

He set the glass down on the table, then stuck two fingers in it and took out another ice cube. As he turned back to face her, her automatic protest died in her throat. She should refuse, tell him to stop, but her hand holding her blouse was pushed aside as if it meant nothing, and again she felt the pleasant shock of the ice against her fevered skin.

She couldn't close her eyes this time; it was too late. Their stares locked; blue to gray, hot to cold, male to female.

He wasn't touching her—only the ice met her skin as he moved it gently across her throat then to her shoulders. He wasn't watching what he was doing—he was watching her, and Charlotte had never had a man look at her so intently.

For the first time, she heard the music coming from the speakers at the end of the room. It sounded like Lena Horne, but who listened to her anymore? As the velvet voice crooned about a man who'd left and rain that never quit, Charlotte took a deep breath.

"I don't normally do this sort of thing."

"I know. You're a nice girl. Right?"

The ice cube had melted, and now his fingers rested lightly at the base of her throat. His eyes continued to burn into her, flaming downward until she felt as if they'd touched the core of her most private thoughts. For two long seconds, she paused then she struggled to sit up, holding her blouse with one shaky hand. "That's right," she said. "And I'd appreciate it if you would try to remember that."

"It might be a lot more fun if we forgot."

For a second, her imagination took off on its own, like a runaway horse, and for the first time in her life Charlotte wondered exactly what it would be like to throw her caution aside, her good sense to the wind. Flustered, she broke his gaze and looked out to the sandy beach outside the screened-in porch. "Is it always this hot?"

He laughed then, a deep rumbling sound that seemed to develop slowly then roll out like building thunder. "If you want hot, you ought to come in August."

With still shaky fingers, she pushed ineffectively at her bangs. "I'll pass, thanks. This feels like hell, if you ask me."

"Oh, no." He shook his head, sipped her iced tea, then frowned as if he'd just drunk anti-freeze. Handing her the glass, he eased to the other end of the couch and reached into the cooler. After pulling out a beer, he sat back, lifting her feet into his lap. "You get used to it—as a matter-of-fact—you'd even get to like it once your blood got a little thinner." He spoke again. "That's the problem with you northerners—your blood's too thick and you wear too many clothes."

He was so incredibly good-looking and unself-conscious that she almost envied him, sitting there wearing only a bathing suit and a tantalizing grin. What would it feel like to be that free, she wondered, to have absolutely no sense of your responsibilities or worries?

Jonathan didn't act that way. Even when they'd snuck off to Cancun one weekend, he'd been so afraid a customer might accidentally see them that they'd done nothing but stay in their room and order meals from downstairs. Well, almost nothing. At least, what *had* happened seemed like nothing.

The mental image of Jonathan woke Charlotte to where she was and what she was doing. She jerked her feet from Sam's lap, sat up abruptly, and set the glass down with a jangle. With shaking fingers, she hastily buttoned her blouse. This man was making her heart beat much too fast. She felt as if she were on her treadmill back home. "I've got work to do," she said in a shaky voice.

He looked at her as if she'd lost her mind. "What's the hurry? Your face is the color of the steamed crab they serve at A.J.'s. Can't it wait while you rest a little longer?"

"I can't sit here all day with my clothes half off and doing nothing."

His slow, easy grin rocked her down to her bare, polished toes. "Would you rather take them *all* off and *do* something?"

"I prefer to get to work," she snapped, her eyes sliding past the warm look in his. "We have business to discuss, and we need to get to it."

Standing up, still shaky but determined not to reveal it, she looked down at her disheveled attire, embarrassed at the weakness of fainting, but even more abashed by his outright sexiness. She *had* to regain control. "Look, I do appreciate all you've done for me, but—"

"But?" His blue eyes drilled her, the single word hanging between them like a thin veil.

"But, frankly we've got one helluva mess on our hands."

TWO

He draped his right arm over the back of the sofa and took a long swallow from the can of beer before speaking in a lazy drawl.

"Maybe *you* have a mess. I don't."

Charlotte's hands tightened at her side, but she resisted the urge to plant her fists on her hips. Jonathan told her she looked foolish when she did that. She straightened her shoulders. "Mr. Gibson, this situation affects us both. I need your full cooperation, or my bank is going to be more upset than it already is."

"And whose fault is that?" Tipping the can once more, he finished the beer then threw the empty toward the trash container in the corner, staring at her all the while. The thump of the aluminum can hitting the plastic sack confirmed his perfect aim and hours of practice.

"It doesn't take a brain surgeon to realize loaning two million dollars and getting nothing but six condos as collateral is not a good idea." He paused, the blue eyes growing speculative. "If I were you, I'd wonder about the yo-yo who approved the loan in the first place."

Charlotte's face flamed. She'd thought the loan would be a low-risk, high-gain one. "It appeared to be a sound business decision at the time," she snapped.

"Oh, yeah? You make it a policy to loan money to people who disappear?"

"If you're referring to Mr. Shilling, we were unaware of his duplicity at the time."

"*Duplicity*? You mean you didn't know he was a crook? Did you expect him to wear a sign?" His blue eyes held hers a moment too long, then he shook his head. "Doesn't matter now, does it? He's in Timbuktu with your two mil, and all you've got is your collateral—six lousy condos in sleepy little Destin."

"That's right—*six, lousy* condos," she said, her temper getting the best of her, "with a leaking roof, a broken sidewalk, and God only knows what else. Why the hell didn't you inform me of their condition?"

From across the room, Charlotte watched as Sam leaned forward. The muscles on his stomach rippled with the movement, reminding her of the smooth waves pounding the sand fifty feet outside their door. His voice curled around her as well. "That's not exactly my responsibility, is it?" He smiled, but his words carried a hint of exasperation.

"We spoke twice, and you *do* own the other half of this project. I would think that during those conversations you might have mentioned—"

"I assumed you knew," he interrupted.

"Even the sidewalk—"

He held up his hand and stopped her. "I know about the sidewalk. Gonna fix it first thing in the morning—"

"Maybe if you spent less time at your 'office' and more time on the job, our investment wouldn't have gone down the tubes."

His eyes tightened into two slits of electric blue, and

Charlotte had to force herself to remain still as he rose slowly to his feet. As he moved closer, the porch seemed to shrink. If only she had on her shoes, she thought illogically, she would be better equipped to handle this infuriating man.

Sam was in the circle of what Charlotte considered her own private space. She wanted to step back, but she stood her ground, reluctant to let him know how intimidated she was. He was so close now she could smell his suntan oil and the lingering beer fumes. "There is no 'our,' Ms. Huntington. I own six. Your bank owns six. That's it. Period. The end," he growled.

She felt, as much as heard, the rumble of his words in the pit of her stomach, but she stood her ground, looking at him straight without a flicker of concern. "I have been authorized by the bank to come here and correct these unfortunate circumstances, to salvage what I can. I'm to remodel the bank's condos and sell them as quickly as possible, but it won't do me any good to repair our side if your side looks like a dump."

A lazy frown drew lines across his forehead. "A dump? I wouldn't exactly call it that."

"Well, I would."

With hardened eyes, he pushed past her and stopped beside the nearest screen panel, raising his arms above his shoulders and grasping the wooden two by fours on either side, staring out at the rolling emerald water. "Do what you want, but don't expect any help from me."

"You own six of these units," she argued, her desperation growing. "I would think you'd want to keep them as perfect as possible."

Dropping his arms to his sides, he swirled around. "I retired two weeks ago from the United States Army, Miss Huntington, and my immediate plans do not include work.'' He spit out the last word as if it were the foulest of obscenities.

Crossing her arms over her chest, Charlotte's realization dawned slowly. She should have recognized the careful way he held his shoulders, the discreet tattoo on his right bicep, but she'd been too distracted.

Sam continued, oblivious to her growing dismay. ''Frankly, I'm not going to lift one damned finger until I'm good and ready. I don't give a flying Philadelphia—''

She held up her hand to stop his oath—that had been one of her father's favorites, and she didn't need Sam to complete the curse to understand what he was saying. ''All right, all right. I'm beginning to get the picture,'' she said wearily.

The hair, she finally decided. His somewhat longish hair had thrown her off. And he was young, too—not over forty-five, at least. She closed her eyes briefly, unable to prevent the small sway in her step.

''You okay?''

His rough voice broke into her thoughts and forced her eyes open. ''I'm fine,'' she said. ''Don't get excited. You're not going to get another opportunity to pull more of my clothes off.''

''Too bad.'' He grinned. ''But even I have to admit, it *would* be more fun if you were awake.''

Her fists found their way to her hips. ''It wouldn't have happened if I'd been awake.''

''I wouldn't place any bets on that, if I were you.''

The humid silence, thick with a tension that Charlotte could taste, was suddenly broken by the *click, click* of the dog's toenails as he strolled onto the porch. Distracted by the irritating sound, Charlotte glanced down and felt her eyes grow wide with disbelief. A muffled snort, sounding suspiciously like an aborted laugh, came from Sam's direction.

The dog continued into the room, stopped at Charlotte's ankles, and then dropped what he'd been carrying so proudly—her left shoe, or more exactly, what was left of her left shoe.

She gasped, cursed, then leaned over to grab the mangled shoe. The dog was faster, however, and in a blink, his jaws recaptured his spoil. In a speedy blur, he disappeared out the doggy door on her left, her shoe going with him.

From behind her, she heard muffled laughter. She swirled and glared at Sam. "What's so damned funny? That dog of yours is disgusting."

"It's not his fault," Sam protested. "He was just having some fun—"

"You're right it's not his fault," she interrupted. "If you hadn't taken such liberties with my clothing, this would never have happened. How can I walk into my hotel without my shoes?"

Sam's smile disappeared as fast as Punch had. "For god's sake, do you really think anyone is going to notice whether or not you've got shoes on? Hell, this is Florida—we don't even wear the rest of our clothes half the time!"

Charlotte's chest heaved with vexation and something else—a tingling awareness of the man standing so close before her, his hands on his hips, his blue eyes looking like fractured pieces of the sky. Suddenly the argument seemed ridiculous—even to her. She dropped her eyes.

"I . . . I guess you're right," she said with a sigh. With a shaky hand, she pulled at the bangs hanging down on her forehead then brushed her fingers over what was left of the French knot at the back of her head. "I must be kinda tired—it's been a long day—and I was just so shocked when I saw the outside . . ."

If she'd been expecting understanding, Charlotte would have been disappointed, but she knew better. This was a military man—an ex-military man. From personal experience, she expected just what she got—a scowl and a low, rumbled "hrumph."

She glanced at her watch. It was almost six p.m. and the only things accomplished had been an argument and the ruination of half her clothing. She walked wearily to the couch, picked up her briefcase and jacket—and one shoe—then turned. Without saying another word, she continued past Sam to the other end of the porch. With her hand on the latch, she paused stiffly. "I'll be back at eight in the morning. Perhaps we can discuss this more professionally at that time."

"Sam? Sam, you in there?"

With a muffled curse, Sam shifted the smoking iron skillet from the front burner to the back and headed for the porch, wiping his hands on the dish towel stuck into his bathing suit. Dinner was practically ready, and the pan was at the perfect temperature—almost as hot as Charlotte had made him.

If this was her at the back door, he'd be tempted to sling her over his shoulder and take her straight to the bedroom. Something about the irritating woman had sent his hormones off the chart—a jump they hadn't felt compelled to take in quite a few years. Totally discombobulated by the realization, Sam strode through the darkened porch like an angry elephant, his heavy steps rattling the furniture as he passed by.

"Yeah?" he growled, opening the door into the night. "What the hell do you want now?"

"Well, you don't have to bite my head off. I can come back tomorrow if that's how the wind's a-blowing."

The tightness in Sam's shoulders eased, and he grinned at the woman who'd been the first of his renters. The special feeling they shared was as close as he'd come to love since his grandmother had died. "Come on in, Myrtle. I thought you were someone else."

Still hesitating, the tiny woman stood on the bottom step. She held up the hem of her voluminous housecoat with one, brown-spotted hand while the other reached for the cigarette dangling from one corner of her mouth. "Well, praise the Lord, I ain't whoever it is. You look mad enough to eat nails—without any salt or pepper."

He held the door open. "You coming in, or you gonna stand there and jaw all night?"

She stepped up and reached for the door, catching it as Sam turned and headed back into the house. "My gawd," she drawled, trailing behind him. "It must be a woman. Nothing can get a man this riled except a woman."

He threw a dirty look over his shoulder but she wasn't looking; she'd bent down to pet Punch, who was cheerfully occupied with destroying the remainder of Charlotte's shoe.

Sam moved the pan back to the front burner and threw in the fillet of snapper he'd already prepared. With a quick cut of his eyes to the still-stooped woman, he threw in the second piece he'd been going to save for lunch.

"How's my favorite doggie in the whole, wide world?" she crooned. "Are you being a good little Punchie?"

"Hah!" Sam snorted. "He's been downright obnoxious today, and I have a feeling I'm going to be paying for it—paying dearly."

Myrtle's faded-blue eyes darted from Sam's face to the drooling dog, the ashes from her cigarette falling between his ears. "And who's gonna deliver the bill? That little lady in black who was looking for you today? The one who stormed out of here?" She took a long drag on her cigarette and squinted at Sam through the haze of smoke. "The one without any shoes on?"

"You noticed that?"

"Yeah—once I got past the blouse that wasn't buttoned straight."

Sam grinned. "Believe me, it's not what you think it is."

Myrtle's cackling laugh ended in an escalating cough. Sam thought he was going to have to hit her on the back, but she finally stopped, waving off the glass of water he stuck under her nose. She lit another cigarette using the butt of the first.

"What kinda lady's man are you, Gibson? God, you could at least let the poor woman get her clothes back on straight."

"You've got it all wrong, Myrtle."

"Sure, sure. All you men say that. My second husband—no, wait, maybe it was my third, or was it, oh, who cares?—one of the bastards I was married to always used that line, too. When a man says that, you know you've got it *exactly* right."

Sam turned from the stove, exasperation lending an even rougher edge to his voice. "Have you eaten dinner?" He tipped the pan toward her so she could see the inside. "You got me so confused I put in too much fish, and I can't eat all this."

"Sure." She grinned around her cigarette. "Just don't cook it till it's rubber, okay?"

Sam rolled his eyes then slammed the pan back on the burner, almost throwing the fish out. Punch looked up hopefully from the last of Charlotte's shoe, then returned to it with a disappointed grunt when nothing came flying toward him.

"So?"

"So what?"

"Who was she? I wanted to ask when she stopped by my place, but I figured it was none of my business."

"And it is now?"

She moved to the sink beside the range and washed her hands, staring at him through narrowed eyes, her mouth pulling on the cigarette as if it were her last. "You brought it up."

Sam sighed. "Her name is Charlotte Huntington. She works for the bank that owns the other half of Safe Harbor."

Myrtle tapped her cigarette on the edge of the sink, crammed it back into the side of her mouth, then started to tear apart the head of lettuce Sam had put out for his salad. Her aging fingers ripped through the leaves, her eyes still on his face. "The fancy ones?"

"Well, they're not so fancy anymore," he said, gently moving the fish in the skillet with the back of a fork. "But, yeah, those."

Myrtle nodded, and Sam tried not to watch as the ashes from her cigarette drifted gently down into the salad. "What's her problem?"

His eyebrows shot up. "How do you know she's got one?"

"She walks like she's got a corncob up her tush."

"And that means she's got a problem?"

"No, that means she's mad. I could hear you yelling at each other—that's how I know she has a problem." She cut her eyes to his. "And it sounds like it's you."

Sam sighed again. "She's mad at the world right now, and I was the closest dog to kick."

She sucked on the cigarette, the ash growing disastrously long. Sam held his breath. The salad was going to taste more like a Camel than lettuce. At the very last second, she turned to grab a tomato and a knife, and the powdery remnants fell to the counter, barely missing the bowl.

"Well, I guess we could all stand a little fixing up.

Actually, that's why I came over. Commode's leaking again.''

"Great." He threw his head back and looked up at the ceiling as if he could find the solution there. "I just replaced that seal last week. What the hell are you throwing down the damned thing, anyway?''

"Nothing you ain't throwing down yours!'' she shot back.

"All right, all right. I'll come over after dinner." His forehead wrinkled and he pulled in his bottom lip. "Is there anything else wrong?''

"Nah—except for that sidewalk, Sam. I swear to God I'm gonna fall down and bust my keister on that board. You gotta—''

He held up his hands. "First thing in the morning, Myrt, I promise." He turned back to the range, grabbed the fork, then lifted the fish to the waiting plates where Myrtle had already dished out the salad. They sat down and started to eat in companionable silence.

Pretending that the small black spots were pepper, Sam separated a larger piece of lettuce from the rest of the salad and chewed slowly, looking at the older woman, but thinking about the younger.

If she'd been ugly, fat, and had a moustache, Charlotte Huntington would have reminded him of a sergeant he once had. Unfortunately, she was none of those. She just had the sergeant's stubbornness and apparent love of rules. Rules! At one time, rules and regulations were the only things that had held Sam together, but not anymore. The last thing he wanted now was a woman whose main goal in life was organizing things. Just the thought of Charlotte Huntington with her briefcase, which he was sure would contain endless lists, was enough to make him cringe.

Reading his mind, Myrtle broke into his thoughts. "You

could handle her with one hand tied behind your back. Just let her know who's the boss and forget about it.''

He grinned, his tension fading. "Don't give me too much credit, now, Myrt. I may get a big head.''

"Well, you're a big fellow, it'd suit ya.'' She pushed back from the table and lit another cigarette, blowing smoke between them like a mosquito fogger, grinning at him all the time.

He stared at her a second longer, then burst into laughter. When he finally got his breath, he spoke, reaching across and grabbing her hand. "Marry me, Myrt—you'll never regret it."

"Hell, no," she snapped and pulled her hand away. "I'm holding out for someone younger."

Charlotte tightened the belt of her robe and stepped out onto the balcony of her hotel room. A warm bath and dinner from room service had done little to ease her concern; Sam Gibson was going to make this task as hard as possible for her, and there wasn't one thing she could do about it.

Her room faced the water, and she could hear the waves, out in the darkness before her, as they hit the shore. *Go home*, they seemed to say, *go home. You can't do any good here.* She shook her head, shoulder-length hair swirling like a cloud around her shoulders. Charlotte Huntington had never quit, and she'd be damned if an aging beach bum thought he could make her do so now.

But the waves continued their argument. *You'll never sell your units with Sam's side looking like it does. What are you going to do about that?*

She reached for one of the small chairs on the balcony and sat down heavily, her eyes still staring at the ground three floors below. A massive pool stretched between the hotel and the beach, and the pale lights surrounding it threw shadows on the sandy shore. Beyond them, the white sand disappeared into an inky blackness, relieved only by dots here and there from other properties. Somewhere down the beach, a faint metal clang repeatedly announced a shift in the wind.

How was she going to fix this problem? Sam obviously didn't care if his condos were less than perfect, but she'd never be able to sell the bank's units while his looked so bad. With the back of her hand, she rubbed her forehead, the small diamond she wore scratching against her skin.

Why didn't she just go home, marry Jonathan, and forget about this whole career business anyway? He'd told her often enough that's what he wanted. That was one of the reasons she'd been so surprised when he'd given her the responsibility of selling the condos. She cradled her left hand in her right and stared at the engagement ring.

What was wrong with her? She'd been telling herself for months that Jonathan was perfect, but without knowing why, she'd been unable to set a date.

He was the kind of man her mother had told her to find, responsible, stable, efficient—everything her father hadn't been. Without even thinking about it, Charlotte knew Jonathan would never disappear for days on end—supposedly "hunting with the boys"—would never come home at three A.M. rowdy and drunk, and would never, ever hide mysterious phone numbers in his coat pocket. He would never do that.

From a distance, the rumble of a motorcycle galvanized her into movement. She stood up slowly, went to the railing, and leaned over as far as she dared, the perfect banker on her mind. So what if bells didn't ring and her toes didn't curl? That only happened in romance novels, didn't it?

The image rose in her mind of the way Sam Gibson had looked at her, bringing with it a shiver of forbidden excitement. That image didn't mean anything, she told herself firmly, but it lodged there in her mind, making her feel curiously disquieted. He was the kind of guy who wouldn't remember your birthday. In fact, he'd probably show up with a bottle of tequila and those hot-blue eyes, and in no time at all make you forget it yourself.

Like a pinprick, the jangling phone beside her bed jerked her back to reality. She ran inside, tripping over her robe, then finally picked up the receiver, breathing hard but trying not to sound like it. "H . . . hello?"

"Charlotte? Is that you?"

A mysterious stab of disappointment ran through her at the sound of Jonathan's slightly nasal tones. She hadn't been expecting Sam Gibson, had she?

"Yes, Jonathan," she answered. "It's me."

"What are you doing?" he said suspiciously. "You sound like you're out of breath."

"I was on the patio. When the phone rang, I had to run inside to catch it."

"Outside? What on earth were you doing out there?"

Charlotte closed her eyes and sat down on the bed. "This is Florida, Jonathan. The weather's quite nice down here—"

"I didn't call you for a meteorological report, Charlotte. I want to know what you got done today."

She tightened her jaw and felt the muscle just beneath her cheekbone twitch. "The flight didn't get in till three, and I went directly to the property."

"Well? What about the condos? Tell me the bank can sell them and get this horrible business behind us."

"They're going to need some work before we actually put them on the market," she admitted, then hesitated. The pause grew even longer as she thought about the major obstacle to that effort—Sam Gibson.

"Well?" he pushed, his exasperated voice going up

another notch. "Are you going to tell me about this, or am I going to have to waste my time asking all the right questions here, Charlotte?"

She jerked herself back to the present. "The units need painting on the outside, the roof looks like it should be replaced, the landscaping is non-existent, and the sidewalk is falling in. I didn't have time to tour the interiors. I'm going to do that tomorrow."

"Didn't have time? My god, you've been there for six hours, Charlotte. I would think you could have done a little more before tucking it in."

Something inside Charlotte snapped. "Give me a break, Jonathan. It's hotter than hell down here—"

"Don't curse," he interrupted. "It's so common."

She drew a deep breath and shut her eyes. Usually she tried to restrain herself around Jonathan, but sometimes the words slipped out before she could stop them. She spoke again, this time keeping her tone more reasonable. "I didn't even have time to change clothes before I left, Jonathan, and I was on a plane all day. To top it off, I passed out in Sam Gibson's condo." She paused; he didn't need all the specifics. "It hasn't been a good day, okay?"

"Passed out?" His voice turned conciliatory. "Are you all right?"

"I'm fine now. It was just the heat." Not to mention a crazed dog, a half-naked man, and more beer fumes than she'd smelled in a long time, she added silently.

"Well, good," he said briskly, obviously happy she wasn't going to dwell on it. "I guess you met him, then?"

"Yes, I found him at, uh, his office." Eyeing the diamond, she rolled her ring around her finger. Why didn't she tell Jonathan the truth? Shaking her head in confusion, she brought her eyes back to the black telephone and the Gideon Bible resting nearby. Her guilt went up another notch.

She rubbed her forehead. "I'll be returning there first thing in the morning. When I know more, I'll call you."

"Please make sure that you do."

Charlotte twisted the phone cord around her hand. "Jonathan?" She hesitated a moment longer then spoke. "Do you miss me?"

His voice was brisk with hard edges. "Don't be ridiculous. Of course, I do. The Stanley account is overdrawn again, and Mr. Stanley is having a fit. The Camerons' trust fund payment was late, and he thinks we owe him some more money . . ."

Charlotte closed her eyes against the litany. Those were not the words she'd wanted—no, needed—to hear, but Jonathan would never understand, even if she could explain. And right now, she wasn't sure she could.

After a curt good-bye, she hung up the phone and wandered back to the patio. Jonathan *was* the man she'd always wanted. Wasn't he? A responsible adult with predictable actions, someone she could always rely on. Her forehead wrinkled as she took a deep breath of salty air. He was a perfect rock of respectability with a sterling character, a long-standing member of St. Martin's Episcopal Church, a board member of the ASPCA, a former boy scout. She could have him anytime she wanted to, so why on earth would she be even looking at another man? Especially someone as bizarre as Sam Gibson with his strange tattoo and his long, wild hair, and those crazy blue, blue eyes?

Gripping the patio railing, she raised her face to the sea breeze, uninvited thoughts pushing their way into her mind like party crashers. Down the beach, the deep rumble of a motorcycle's engine roared briefly then faded into the night.

Sam Gibson was not her kind of man. So why couldn't she stop thinking about him?

THREE

The Gulf breeze caressed her face with a sensual finger of warmth as Charlotte stepped outside the next morning. The salty taste of the air, the dull roar of the waves hitting the shore behind the hotel, the sight of a sea gull riding the currents far above her, all seemed to combine and tell her to take the day off, but she turned to the rental car and kept going. She had work to do.

Through a windshield dulled by sea air, she glared at the offending project when she arrived twenty minutes later. Like missing teeth, dark blotches stained the wide expanse of roof. How long had the shingles been absent? Working her way down, Charlotte cataloged peeling gray paint, missing window screens, and a dark-green awning that had come loose and was now flapping wildly against the weathered wood. Someone had leaned a ladder against the wall as if to fix the flying cover, but had gotten no further. At the other end, two palm trees, their lower fronds brown and shaggy, stood like lonely sentinels above flower beds filled with wild sea grasses. A battered picnic table completed the al fresco dining area.

There was so much to do she didn't even know where to start. Reaching for her daily notebook, she sighed and opened it up to the page bearing Tuesday's date. Taking the pen from the side pocket, she bent closer and started to write. Her concentration was so intense, her attention so complete, that she didn't even see the tiny, gray-haired man until he was standing beside her car window, rapping on the glass with gnarled knuckles.

The angry knocking stole Charlotte's breath, and her pen zigzagged off the page in a scribble of surprise, her startled gaze flying to the window. Through the sea-sprayed glass, an older man whose head barely cleared the top of the car glared at her. The frown he wore wrinkled his entire face, and bushy eyebrows drew a fierce line over his darting black eyes. He shook one brown-spotted fist at her window and motioned for her to roll down the glass.

With some misgivings, she opened the window. "May I help you?" she asked in a tentative voice.

"Whatchu doing here?" He gestured wildly toward her notebook, then pointed to his eyes. "I see you writing. I know you here to take me back, but I not go. Hokay? You get that straight, lady."

Charlotte's heart began to pound. He couldn't have been over five foot two, but he presented a very wild picture. Long, dark hair, streaked with grey, stood out from his head and a straggly Fu Manchu moustache and beard added to his strange appearance. He looked Oriental, but something about his accent sounded almost like Spanish. As she stared, his voice went up another decibel, and her hand eased toward the lock on her car door.

"I no go back, don't give DAMN what you say."

At the sound of his now totally enraged voice, Charlotte pressed back against the leather of her car seat, desperate for a way out of the situation. The old man was too small to be much of a threat, but what he lacked in stature, he made up for in volume. His harangue continued unabated and even louder. Just as she was about to start the car and simply drive away, the tall form of Sam Gibson rounded one end of the condos. She never expected to be happy to see him, but a wave of relief washed over her as he slowly approached the car.

"Juan, Juan. What's the trouble here?"

The old man's speech stopped abruptly, and the look in his black eyes as he gazed up at Sam stopped Charlotte as well. She'd never seen such blind trust and adoration.

"Sam," he said in an undertone, cutting his eyes toward Charlotte. "I see this woman out here. She's— *como se dice?*—suspicious, no?"

A rapid-fire Spanish conversation ensued, Charlotte staring with amazement up at Sam, then down at the old man. Finally, the old man puckered his lips, stared doubtfully at her once more, then ambled off, pulling a rake behind him. Sam leaned down to look in the window at her.

"Who in the world was that?" she asked, her voice squeaky with relief. "He scared me half to death."

Sam grinned at her then looked over at the tiny figure, now stabbing his rake viciously over the sea grass at the far end of the parking lot. As they watched, his head moved this way and that, a silent conversation going on with an imaginary companion.

"That's Juan Kayota, he's one of my tenants," he answered. "He's also the gardener."

"Gardener?" Charlotte felt her eyes go wide. "You trust him with sharp implements?"

Sam chuckled then opened her car door and held out his hand. She shot another quick look at Juan, but he was totally absorbed in his shadowy discussion. Accepting Sam's fingers, she stepped outside the car.

"I don't seem to recall anything in the paperwork about Safe Harbor having any employees," she said.

"I pay his salary—it gives him a little extra and makes him feel useful."

She looked up into Sam's blue eyes, her opinion of him adjusting slightly, like a subtle shift in the sands. "What's wrong with him?" she asked.

"Nothing." He slammed the door behind her, and they started toward the units. "He's old, that's all. On occasion, he still thinks immigration's after him, but he's legal. He got his citizenship years ago, but sometimes he forgets."

They'd reached the sidewalk. "Forgets? How can you forget something like that?"

Sam laughed easily, a low rumble that echoed the sound of the waves behind the condos. "Come on, sweetheart, he's eighty-eight."

She stared at the bent-over figure. "But what about his family? Where are they?"

Sam shrugged and put back on the dark sunglasses he'd been holding. "He hasn't got any. He's outlived them all."

"So you take care of him?"

"Yeah, I guess you could say that. I keep an eye on him, just to make sure he's doing okay."

Today, a pair of faded-blue shorts were Sam's only attire; his feet were bare and so was his head. Lifting his hand to his chest, Sam idly threaded his fingers through the curly hair, his eyes focusing on the older man. In the bright sunlight of the morning, Charlotte could see streaks of silver she hadn't noticed before. Somehow, he didn't seem like he'd be the type of man to look after a lonely, old bachelor.

She forced herself back to the task at hand. "Thank you for your help. I guess that's the second time you've rescued me."

"That's okay." His blue eyes were narrowed against the blazing Florida sun. "I like rescuing you."

Warmth that had nothing to do with the Florida sun flooded her, and she let a small smile escape despite the ripple of unease going down her back.

He turned and continued down the sidewalk, Charlotte struggling to keep up with his long strides. He pointed to the broken board as they passed. "Going to fix that first thing in the morning. Watch your step."

"Thank you," she said primly. "It's already on my list."

They stopped outside the door of the first unit, and Sam reached for the keys she held in her hand. His fingers lingered a second longer on hers than was completely necessary, and when she looked at him, his smile was lazy, wide, and knowing.

She blushed automatically because . . . well, just because, she thought illogically. He made it impossible for her to concentrate; all her senses were busy dealing with the smell of coconut oil, the sight of tanned skin, and the sexy come-ons he seemed to delight in.

Finally, he turned to the door. After a moment's struggle with the stubborn key, the lock opened, and they walked inside. Navigating competently through the darkened rooms, Sam went to the opposite end of the unit and pulled back the drapes. Outside, blinding sunlight reflected off the ocean then bounced back into the room to flood the gloomy interior. Charlotte stepped gingerly into the center of the musty smelling den.

"The units all pretty much have the same floor plan," Sam said. "This is a one-bedroom, but there are two- and three-bedroom units, too."

"Why does it smell so bad?"

He walked to the glass-topped table between the den and the kitchen bar and ran his finger over the dusty top.

"No one's been in here for months. They haven't been cleaned, and in Florida, you've got to keep stuff up, or it doesn't last long."

She raised her eyebrows, but stayed silent.

"Yes," he said lazily. "I do know that fact. And, as soon as I've enjoyed my retirement as much as I can stand it, I'm going to tackle the outside repairs—but not before. I waited a helluva long time to retire, and I'm going to savor every minute of it."

In the dim light of the condo, Charlotte studied Sam's face. He was standing closer to her than she would have liked, but the proximity allowed her to examine him even more intently. The planed cheeks were smooth this morning, the eyelids taut, the mouth still full and promising. How could he have retired so young?

He stepped closer, his lips parting in a slow smile as he obviously read the question in her eyes. "I was an early starter," he said, pausing long enough to make her wonder if he meant that in *all* the possible ways. With a hard swallow, she realized he probably did.

He reached out and took a strand of her hair between his fingers then rubbed it back and forth as if he were judging fine silk. "And I'm going to have one helluva finish, too," he said, smiling even wider. "Why don't you stick around and watch?"

Charlotte jerked her hair out of his hand and stepped back, watching him warily. He tilted his head. "What's wrong? Scared of a decrepit, old retiree?"

Her heart in her throat, Charlotte sidestepped the question. "You're not that old."

"I'm forty-five," he replied. "That must seem old to a sweet, young thing like you."

"I'm over thirty, Mr. Gibson."

"And still ambitious."

"What's wrong with that? I have a career, and there are things I have to accomplish if I want to get ahead."

"Ahead of what?"

"I beg your pardon?" She stared at him, mesmerized by his steady stare.

"What is it you want to get ahead of?" he said patiently. "Another bank, another job, another woman?"

She flicked her tongue over her lips. Her mouth felt as if she'd swallowed sand for breakfast.

"I . . . I want to be successful," she finished lamely.

"And successful is . . ." He waited for her to finish.

"Successful is getting these condos in condition to be sold," she said briskly, desperate to end this ridiculous conversation. "Now, please tell me why you haven't taken care of them, Mr. Gibson?"

He stared at her as though weighing her answer and finding it lacking. Apparently deciding to ignore the deficiency, he answered with his own question. "Why don't you call me Sam?"

"All right, Sam," she replied awkwardly. "Surely you have a sound reason for letting your investment deteriorate. I'd like to know what it is."

He brushed past her and walked into the kitchen. "Aren't you forgetting something?"

She watched him open the refrigerator, look inside, then slowly close the door again. "Like what?"

He leaned against the appliance and crossed his arms. "I don't own these. Your bank does."

"But what about the outside? Your end is just as run-down as ours is."

"Not that it's any business of yours, Ms. Huntington, but I purchased these condos knowing what their condition was—which is more than I can say for your bank."

Her face flushed in the heated apartment, but the redness had nothing to do with the temperature. "The man we gave the loan to—Robert Shilling—bribed the appraiser into giving us a false report. We thought they were in perfect shape until we took them over.'' She twisted her diamond ring. ''I didn't realize how badly they'd deteriorated until I arrived, however.''

''Deteriorated!'' His eyes opened wide. ''You keep using that word, but they're not that bad. These particular ones are dirty, need a new coat of paint, some new carpeting, maybe wallpaper that doesn't look like it came from a Holiday Inn built in 1964, but I wouldn't say they're deteriorating.''

''What about the exterior?''

''What's the hurry? I don't like to be rushed.'' Their eyes locked. ''Some people like it fast,'' he continued, his stare reaching inside to stroke her private thoughts, ''but I've always thought slow was better.'' He smiled innocently. ''Don't you agree?''

Charlotte swallowed past the knot that had suddenly developed in her throat, but stayed silent as he came around the corner of the bar. Again, the scent of coconut oil wafted toward her. ''Would you like to see the bedroom?'' he asked.

''Fine,'' she answered stiffly.

He stared at her a minute longer, then walked slowly down a hall to the right of the den. She followed his broad, bare back, her own spine ramrod straight.

The room was dim, the sunlight held at bay by the dusty drapes. In the center was a king-sized bed. On the ceiling above it were squares of decorative mirror.

''Oh, my,'' she said automatically, her fingers twisting her diamond ring. ''Th . . . that's interesting.''

He followed her gaze to the ceiling. ''Yeah. We get a lot of newlyweds down here. They seem to like that kind of thing.'' He stepped closer and picked up her hand to look at her ring. "What's your man got planned for *your* honeymoon?"

He covered her diamond with the flat of his thumb, moving the ring back and forth across her finger. The simple touch of his hand against hers was unbearably exciting, and she jerked her fingers away, trying to make her voice frosty as she answered. She didn't succeed. "I don't think Jonathan . . . well, I've never, uh, slept in a bed with mirrors over it." She stopped, holding back a groan of despair at her inept answer. "What keeps them up there?" she said, searching for a way to get past the awkward moment.

The gleam in his eyes turned speculative. "Think you and Jonathan might shake them down?"

Her face instantly flamed. There was definitely no chance of that with Jonathan. "Well, of course not. I just meant, well . . . I just wondered if it was safe, that's all."

"We could give it a test if you like," he said, his warm stare starting at her face and going down her body before coming slowly back up. "For the bank's records, of course—"

"Helloooo. Sam, are you in there?"

Charlotte's head jerked around with relief toward the high-pitched voice calling from the kitchen.

"Back here, Sissy. We're in the bedroom." He grinned and looked down at Charlotte. "Prepare yourself. These are two more of my tenants. They're sisters, and the only hundred-year-old virgins left."

Before she could react, two women rounded the corner, arguing between them, each talking at the same time.

"I told you he's been on the beach before, Sissy. If you knew how to operate those binoculars properly, you'd have recognized him. We saw him last Saturday."

"Oh, you're mistaken, Margaret. I know he's new. I would have remembered that bright orange bathing suit and those legs, believe me, I would have recognized—oh, hello! And who is this?"

The shorter of the two women smiled brightly at Charlotte, her eyes blinking rapidly behind enormous, thick glasses. Her hair was frizzy and gray, her smile looked perpetual, and the shorts covering her thin, tanned legs were long and baggy.

Beside her stood a much taller, more severe-looking woman. Her hair was twisted into a neat bun at the back of her head and a large straw hat adorned her head, its brim properly turned at a precise angle. She, too, wore shorts, but they were pale pink. Tucked neatly inside the waistband was a pink-and-white striped camp shirt.

"Miss Sissy and Miss Margaret, may I present Miss Charlotte Huntington."

A hint of lavender reached Charlotte's nose as they each moved closer to take her hand. Their skin felt dry and fragile, like pages from an old book.

"You must be that silly woman from the bank who fainted yesterday. Myrtle told us about you."

The taller woman gasped. "Sissy, watch your tongue, for heaven's sake."

"Well, don't get your knickers in a twist. I was just repeating what Myrtle said—it doesn't mean that's what I think." She turned to stare myopically at Charlotte. "She looks okay to me."

Surprisingly, Charlotte found herself more amused than insulted, and she returned the grin.

Margaret shook her head. "Don't pay any attention to Sissy, my dear. She's not as nutty as she sounds."

Sam stepped closer to Sissy and with a protective movement, put his arm around her, his eyes boring into Charlotte's.

"Charlotte *is* okay, Sissy. She's just not used to Florida yet."

Pursing her scarlet lips, the older woman nodded. "Well, I can certainly understand that. But Florida has room for everyone."

"It is a big state," Charlotte agreed.

"Oh, no, sweetie, that's not what I mean."

Intrigued, Charlotte stared and waited for her to finish. She wasn't disappointed.

"I meant everyone can do his own thing here. It's practically guaranteed in the state's constitution. Florida's got a long history of individualism, everybody fighting to have his way or nothing. Why, they argued so long about secession that the poor governor killed himself at the end of the war."

Sam, who'd been staring at the short woman tucked under his arm, looked up proudly. "Miss Sissy was a history teacher down in Pensacola before she retired."

"That's right," she said. "Oldest city in the state."

Margaret put her hands on her hips. "Why, Sissy, you ole liar, you. You know St. Augustine is older than—"

With a grin, Sam broke in once more. "Miss Margaret was, too."

Charlotte nodded politely while the two sisters continued to argue. Finally, they turned around and left, their discussion still going strong as they stepped out the front door. Two seconds later, Margaret returned, slightly out of breath.

"Sam, I almost forgot—can you come by this afternoon and work on the sink? I think it's plugged up again. Sissy probably threw last night's shrimp shells down it, even though I've told her a hundred times not to."

"Sure," he said. "Don't worry about it. I'll be there after lunch."

She smiled, nodded to Charlotte then breezed out again. Charlotte turned back to Sam, feeling as if she'd just been sucked into a geriatric tornado.

"Shall we look at the rest of the units?" he asked innocently.

She followed him outside, pausing as he locked the unit. "Are all of your tenants, um . . ."

"Old?"

"Well, yes—old?" Actually, she'd wanted to say "nuts," but that didn't sound very polite.

"Yeah, they are." He rattled the doorknob once to check the lock then turned, wearing a sweet smile that lifted his full lips and crinkled the dark skin around his eyes. "But I love 'em. My grandparents raised me, and I guess I've got a soft spot for old people. You have to if you live in Florida, that's for sure."

He obviously felt as if his tenants were his family. "Are your grandparents still alive?" she asked.

"No. I lost them several years ago. How about yours? Are they—"

Charlotte shook her head regretfully, feeling the loss she always felt when other people talked about their families with such love in their voices. "Actually, I never knew them very well. My parents divorced when I was a teenager."

He nodded, obviously understanding her unstated regrets, but before he could say more, his eyes went to a man and woman walking down the sidewalk. "Here come Paul and Louise. I'll introduce you to them. They're a little more conventional."

A second later, Charlotte was shaking the tanned and leathery hand of Paul Smith. His wife, Louise, looked on with a smile.

Paul Smith had silver wings on either side of his temples and bright blue eyes. Tilted back on his head was a cap that had "Sandestin" written across the front. "We're going for eighteen holes this morning, Sam. Sure you don't want to come along?"

"Can't today, Paul. I appreciate the invite, but Charlotte and I have some stuff—uh, work—to do. I'll catch you next time."

The older man looked at Charlotte with curiosity. "Work? That's a dirty word around here, Miss Huntington. How in the world did you get Sam to say it?"

"It wasn't easy," she replied drily.

He nodded once as if he really understood.

"Do you golf, Charlotte?" Louise asked.

Charlotte turned to Paul's wife. She wore a generous smile and the biggest diamond Charlotte had ever seen. "No—I've never had the time."

"Well, we've got to change that." Paul smiled and took his wife's arm, obviously anxious to get to the greens. "Maybe tomorrow."

They hurried off, Charlotte and Sam watching as they got into a gray Cadillac and pulled out onto the highway.

"They seem like nice people," Charlotte said.

"You mean normal?"

She looked up at Sam. "Well . . ."

He grinned once more then led her into the next condo. An hour later, they emerged from the last one. She was shocked at the amount of work they all needed, and said so as Sam led her to a nearby picnic table. They both sat down.

"They could stand a little touching up," he agreed.

"A little?" Charlotte said. "How can you say that? The interiors look awful, and the outside is even worse." She tapped the notebook she'd been carrying. "I was making my preliminary list of the problems on the exterior when Juan interrupted me. If I hadn't stopped, it would be a mile long."

"Thank God for Juan," Sam muttered, twirling his sunglasses between wide fingers.

Charlotte pursed her lips. "I've got to get the units

ready as soon as possible, or I'll miss the summer buyers. Face it, Sam, we have a lot of work to do and not much time.''

Sam dropped the glasses to the rough cedar, his eyes narrowing as he rumbled one word. ''We? I thought I made myself clear yesterday. I don't intend to help.''

''B . . . but I can't repair my side and leave your side alone.''

''Why not?''

Patience was not Charlotte's strong suit, but she tried once more. ''Condo owners have to be in agreement about repairs to the exterior of the units.'' She swept her hand out to indicate the units. ''Look at them. Do you really think I can sell my units if yours look like hell?''

''For a woman who wears fancy underwear, your vocabulary's awfully blunt.''

With a sharp intake of breath, Charlotte glared at Sam, her irritation covering her embarrassment as she leaned forward. ''My vocabulary *and* my underwear are not the topics of discussion here. I would appreciate it if you wouldn't speak of such private things.''

Before she could pull away, he put his hand over hers and leaned closer. Their noses were inches away, and Charlotte noticed for the first time that he had a tiny scar near the edge of his left eyebrow. She tried to reclaim her fingers, but he tightened his grip and smiled. ''Underwear isn't private. Spending all afternoon in bed, making long, slow love till you think you've died, cooling off in the hot tub, and starting all over again—now *that's* private.''

At his words, a liquid warmth started in the pit of her stomach then spread lower as he turned her hand over and traced the lines in her palm. She shivered as if his rough, brown fingers were touching the inside of her thigh instead of the inside of her hand. She jerked away and stood up.

He laughed, a wicked, provoking sound, as she whirled

away and went to her car, her apricot blush darkening her face. He was insufferable, she fumed, fumbling with the keys, then stopping to lean against the car and catch her breath. Insufferable; yes, but more exciting than any man she'd ever met in her life.

FOUR

It wasn't much of a bathing suit; only two little patches at the top shaped like shells and a third one, only slightly larger, at the bottom. The back was a thong that looked mighty uncomfortable. From behind dark glasses, Sam watched the young girl sway down the beach and thought momentarily of asking her if it *was* uncomfortable. He finally decided to keep quiet. Women seemed to be awfully sensitive when you asked them about their clothes.

At least Charlotte Huntington was. And that, of course, was exactly why he'd said what he did about her underwear. Something about that woman made him want to torment her.

He reached behind him and dug into his cooler. At his side, Punch growled over the disturbance then resettled as Sam turned back around, the cold beer in his hand. "What's the matter, boy?" he asked. "She got you in a bad mood, too?"

Popping the tab, Sam leaned back into his chair, the umbrella over his head snapping in the stiff breeze, the waves curling fast and furiously in front of him. He'd been on the beach since seven that morning. Started with coffee and a slightly stale piece of Myrtle's pound cake but had moved on at lunchtime to beer and a baloney sandwich. His condo sat only a couple of hundred feet behind him, but once Sam was settled in, he hated to go back for anything. It was easier to plan ahead.

Just like he'd planned his whole life. Organization had been the only defense a ten year old could muster against death and disaster, and it'd served him well following his parents' deaths. Their car had wrapped around a tree on a rainy night, and he'd been jerked from a typical middle-class childhood to a farm in rural Idaho to live with grand-parents he'd seen only at Christmas until then. It'd been a terrible change; he'd even run away several times, but eventually he'd grown to love them.

As soon as he could, though, he'd joined the army. He'd needed that sense of order, that strict regimentation the military had offered. And on the various bases where he'd lived, he'd found another family—the men of his squad.

Even then, however, he'd held back a piece of himself, feeling that if he gave too much, he'd lose too much. The shell he built became impenetrable, protected by rules and fortified by organization.

He'd had his share of affairs, of course, but none had ever reached his heart—if you didn't count Jolene, and he always tried not to.

Yes, the military had been his entire life, until this spring. Now he was free, and for the first time in his forty-five years he didn't have—or want—the stringent rules, the unbending protocols, the high standards. He had to do only what he wanted to do and nothing more.

Obviously, Charlotte Huntington had other plans. Staring out at the emerald waves, he gulped half the beer.

Why? Why now? Why her? Why him? Hadn't he fought life long enough?

He was happy, his tenants were happy—well, *most* of them were. And the repairs would all get done in good time. As soon as he'd had the opportunity to wind down a little, he'd get right on them. But not now.

No, now he wanted to fish all day and lie in the sun, not worry about whether or not he had to go haul some soldier out of jail for beating up his wife. Now he could wear bathing suits with his hair long and feet bare, instead of uniforms with jackets and shirts and matching hats on top of hair trimmed too close for comfort.

He closed his eyes against the glare on the water, but Charlotte's face came into his mind, and he couldn't close his eyes to that. She was so damned prim and proper, all he could think about was running his hands through her hair and wrinkling those crisp clothes she seemed to prefer.

She was trouble, pure and simple, representing all the list-making and order-taking he'd had to do for the past twenty years. Nothing, especially Charlotte Huntington, was going to drag him back into the regimentation he'd just escaped.

So why couldn't he stop thinking about huge silver eyes that looked like the sky just before the sun came up and rich coffee-colored hair that stuck in tendrils to damp skin?

Sam moaned, his fingers tightening around the now-empty can of beer. Why her?

The restaurant was a small one with wooden picnic tables outside. Charlotte gave the waitress her dinner order, then leaned her elbows on the table and ignored the pile of paperwork she'd brought with her. She looked instead at the pier directly to her right where the gentle lap of water against hulls lulled her into forgetting about the deed restrictions, city codes, and property requirements she'd just picked up from a local real estate agent.

With her chin resting on her hands, Charlotte stared at the fishing boats. Almost every one of them had a small wooden stand and table on the pier directly in front of it, complete with a sign declaring its expertise in snagging the biggest and the best. Behind the nearest table, a teenager, his left hand protected by a steel mesh glove, bent over and removed a three-foot-long fish from a nearby cooler. From his right hand, the sudden flash of honed steel caught the sinking sun's rays. Charlotte sipped her drink and watched him sharpen the deadly knife on a well-used whetstone, then in a ballet of astonishing speed and dexterity, the youngster proceeded to clean and gut the huge fish.

Mesmerized, Charlotte stared at his flying hands until he paused and raised his head as someone from the restaurant's bar called out his name. Upward, to the deck on the roof of the low building where the bar was situated, she followed the young boy's smile, sharply pulling in her breath as she saw the man who'd called out. It was Sam.

Something about Sam Gibson was so intriguing, so fascinating, that Charlotte couldn't resist an opportunity to stare without his knowledge. She brought her glass to her lips and gawked unabashedly. He had the kind of presence which few men ever develop, but for which many strive—an almost overwhelming virility.

Sun-streaked hair, darkened by the evening sun and ruffled by the soft sea breeze, framed his chiseled face, and even from a distance the sparkle of his blue eyes reached her. His snug black T-shirt reminded her of the hard chest she'd fallen against that first day, and she could almost smell the sharp fumes of the beer he gripped in his right hand. As she continued to watch, a group of laughing friends—men and women—swallowed him, pulling him back into the center of the deck, lost to her sight.

They looked as if they were having a lot of fun, and just for a moment, Charlotte wished she were up there, too. The women wore bright sundresses that showed off their tans, and men stood beside them circling their waists with arms, strong and brown. The music picked up, and several couples started to dance. Instantly, Charlotte imagined how it would feel to have Sam's arms around her, swaying in the cool sea breeze but feeling warmer than ever. Resolutely, she shook the thought from her head. She was engaged, for heaven's sake, to another man—a far more respectable, reliable, upstanding man than Sam Gibson would ever be. Sighing, she turned back to her table.

With little interest, Charlotte picked at the wilting greens in the salad the waitress had brought. Just as she stabbed a solitary tomato, a hugh black Labrador strolled up to her table, his dark eyes moving between her plate and her face in dignified supplication. Recognizing a soft touch when he saw one, he lowered his haunches and sat down beside Charlotte's bench in a move that said he had all the time in the world.

"Why not?" Charlotte said with a dry grin. "You look like you could use a friend, too." She pulled the tomato off the tines of her fork and leaned over, offering the morsel to the dog with her fingers. With great modesty, he inclined his head and daintily peeled back his lips, accepting her gift as if it were his right. Concentrating solely on the dog, she didn't see Sam until he was already sitting down at her table.

"You better watch out. In places like these, you never know what kind of animal you'll find," he teased.

She jerked her head up, one hand against her temple to pull the hair from her eyes. "I'm not too worried," she said, her heart thumping against her chest as if it wanted to escape. "He looks pretty tame."

Sam grinned and sipped from his beer, his eyes never leaving hers. "Looks can be deceiving."

I don't think so, she thought silently. *You look like the devil himself, and I think that's exactly who you are.*

Grateful for the waitress's interruption as she placed a platter of fried shrimp on the table between them, Charlotte smiled tightly and pointed to the plate. "Have you eaten? If you haven't, I'd be happy to share."

"Thanks." He smiled slowly and reached out with sun-baked fingers, taking one of the shrimp then biting into it. "My friends and I haven't gotten around to eating yet. We've been too busy catching up."

Charlotte nodded then took a shrimp of her own. "I saw you on the deck," she said, tilting her head toward the roof. "Catching up on what?"

"Old times, new times, whatever." He shrugged as if it weren't important, but Charlotte immediately got the impression it was. He obviously felt very close to them. "They're people I knew from the military. Most of them are still in, and they're giving me the scoop on everything that's changed."

She automatically tightened her lips, her eyes swinging upward at a sudden burst of raucous laughter. "That probably won't take long," she said, her voice more bitter than she intended. "In the military life, some things are *always* the same."

As his blue eyes narrowed in sudden concentration to study her, Charlotte bit the inside of her lip but stayed silent. She felt like a porcupine with its bristles up, but it was too late now. She'd already spoken and something told her Sam wouldn't let up 'til he knew more. His next words confirmed her fears.

He reached out for another shrimp. "And just what do *you* know of the military life?"

She swallowed hard then raised her eyes defiantly. "Enough to know that the drinking, partying, and lying never end."

He chewed slowly, his eyes never leaving her face. "That's a pretty broad condemnation," he said, his voice more neutral than his eyes. "Can you back it up?"

"Unfortunately, yes. My father was in the military all his life—short as it was. I know firsthand what it means to be an army brat, believe me."

"I take it, then, you didn't enjoy it."

"Not one minute of it. My mother didn't either. That's why they divorced when I was a teenager. She went her way, and he went his. Two years later, he'd been kicked out of the army. The next year, he was dead."

Sam's eyes widened almost imperceptibly. "And you blame his death on the stress of being discharged?"

"No," she said flatly. "I blame his discharge on his drinking. I blame his death on him." She paused, her eyes going to the sun as it disappeared over the water. "It was his hand on the gun."

"I'm sorry." He paused then continued quietly, the music in the background strangely juxtaposed with the conversation. "I can't quite agree with your conclusions, though. There are a lot of fine people in the military who don't fit the picture you just drew."

"Maybe," Charlotte finally answered, her reluctance obvious, "but I haven't met any." With one fingernail, she traced a fine line in the wood of the table, part of her willing to agree but part of her still listening to her mother's long-held arguments. *You make sure you do better than me, Charlotte. Stay away from soldiers, and find a respectable man, you hear?*

He reached across the table and captured her nervous

fingers. Her hands were cold with anxiety, but his were warm and reassuring. "What about me?" he teased. "I'm a fine, upstanding citizen, a hard worker, sober—"

She had an instant of wishing desperately that he was telling the truth, because if he was all those things, she could see herself falling for him—falling deeper and deeper than any woman had a right to. She forced herself, however, to look past the good looks and silver tongue.

"Right," she suddenly interrupted, her breath coming faster at his touch. "And that's why I found you, and your beer cans, on the beach in front of a condo project that's so neglected I can't even sell half of it."

His grip tightened, but his smile stayed in place. "Relaxing doesn't mean you're worthless. Neither does drinking. It's when you can't control either that you get into trouble."

"And you can?"

"Absolutely. The only thing you shouldn't be able to control is your passion."

Their eyes, and their hands, locked over the table, and a tremor of temptation skittered over Charlotte's back. Passion wasn't something she'd been told was important in a man, but she knew that was exactly what Jonathan lacked and Sam possessed. Her breath caught in her throat. Was passion what she'd been searching for? She'd done what her mother had told her to—found a *respectable* man—yet, it just didn't feel *right*. Respectable, yes; exciting, no. Not like the man holding her hand now, the man who was sending tingling sensations right up her arm and down into her belly, just by closing his fingers around hers—fingers that wore another man's ring.

Charlotte jerked her hand away as if Sam had just set fire to her nails, her thumb twisting Jonathan's diamond around and around.

Sam leaned back, stared at her a moment longer, then

caught the waitress's eye and pointed to his beer. She nodded once and disappeared toward the bar.

Suddenly, Charlotte was anxious to be alone again, to disappear back into the solitude she'd been cursing earlier. At least there, she didn't have to face this strange restlessness Sam seemed to impart to her. "Won't your friends be missing you?" she asked with a nod over her shoulder.

"I'll catch up with them later," he said casually, smiling his thanks as the waitress reappeared. "I'd like to hear more about you. Tell me more about your family. Do you have any brothers or sisters?"

Charlotte swallowed hard. She was flattered by his attention, but more nervous than she'd ever been around a man. Sam had that effect on her. "One brother," she finally answered. "He's stationed in Germany."

Sam grinned. "So, there is at least one person in the military you like, right?"

She returned his smile with some hesitation. "I . . . I wouldn't, well—actually, we don't get along too well, either."

"That's a shame," he said, his eyes speculative. "I would have killed for a brother when I was younger."

"You had none?"

He shook his head. "My parents died in a car crash when I was just a kid. That's why my grandparents raised me." His broad shoulders shrugged, then he continued. "I don't know—even if I'd had a brother, we'd probably fight anyway."

"I wouldn't know," she said stiffly. "Mine was never around to fight with—he and Dad were always off together—fishing, hunting. Whatever it is that fathers and sons do by themselves all the time that women can't participate in."

Sam's forehead wrinkled, but he kept his question to himself, as if he sensed her reluctance to say more. He wrapped his hands around the beer and looked out over the pier. "Well, seems like I do best with people that are over seventy, anyway, if you want to know the truth."

She watched him reach out for another shrimp, then did what she'd promised herself she wouldn't—compared him again with the man who'd given her the ring she now twisted once more. Sam was so alive, so involved in everything, that he made Jonathan look like the wax to his flame. She had no illusions about which man would keep her warmer, either. Her thoughts strayed, taking paths they shouldn't, only to be pulled back by Sam's puzzled look. She realized then he was repeating a question he'd obviously already asked once.

"Why don't you join me and my friends?" He inclined his head toward the bar. "Looks like they want to move on." He rose slowly from the table and held out his hand. "Come on. You need a little fun."

Charlotte covered her left hand with her right, Jonathan's diamond biting into the soft palm of her hand. At the moment, there was nothing she wanted more than to jump up and place that palm into Sam's larger one, but years of discipline held her back. Her work was waiting, she had phone calls to return and papers to study. And Jonathan would be calling to make sure she'd done it all.

"I . . . I'd love to," she finally answered, "but I've—"

"Got to work," he finished.

She pulled her bottom lip in between her teeth, knowing a narrow line now furrowed her brow. "That's right. I haven't done as much as I should, and . . ."

The soft lights along the pier glinted gold sparks off his hair as he bent down, ignoring the rowdy calls of his friends. His face inches from hers, Sam shot her through with a frighteningly blue stare then twisted one hand into her windswept hair, his thumb rough along the line of her jaw. "You need to loosen up, sweetheart. You're not your father, you know."

She stiffened at his words, despite the warmth of his touch. "What exactly does that mean?"

His fingers tightened in her hair as if he wanted to remember the silky feeling later. "It means that you can have a good time and relax occasionally, and still stay in control."

Before she could bring herself to speak, he swiftly pressed his lips against hers then left—left her breathless.

The thought of returning to an empty hotel room after dinner was more than Charlotte could face and, when she pulled her car out of the restaurant's parking lot, she found herself heading instead for the condos. She got there in a few minutes and, after killing the engine of her car, she climbed out and strolled to the forlorn picnic table where she and Sam had sat earlier that day after she'd toured the condos. In the orangey light of the overhead street lamp, the area looked more unkempt and shabby than ever.

If she looked past the table, however, and down to the beach, the beauty of the night made her heart ache. It was a night for lovers. A pale silver light lined the edge of the sea as the moon rose over the horizon.

The beach was deserted, echoing her own lonely state. In the distance, she heard again the throaty call of a motorcycle's engine. Staring at the water's edge, she saw that Sam had already taken down the umbrellas and chairs and tucked them into the white wooden shelter at the edge of the dunes. In the bare light, only the confusion of a thousand footprints, like faint memories, told Charlotte that the sugar-white sand had been visited today.

She sank to the cedar bench, the evening wind picking up her hair and tossing it with casual disregard around her shoulders. From behind the condos, came the roar of the waves, and she breathed deeply. The tangy ocean air held the promise of the night—a hot, sultry promise that was an empty one for Charlotte. She stared at the unfilled place across the table. Where had Sam and his friends gone, she wondered. To another bar, to someone's house, to each other's beds? She blinked as a strand of dark hair whipped into her eyes, then pulled the silky curl back with a trembling hand. Why did she care who Sam might be loving tonight?

The ringing phone pulled at Charlotte's consciousness like a nagging toothache. Ignoring the insistent demand was impossible. Finally, groggily, she reached for it and managed to send the entire machine crashing off the nightstand. With a muffled curse, she stretched over the edge of the bed and retrieved the receiver, using the cord to pull it to her as if she were reeling in a fish.

"Hell . . ." she stopped and cleared her throat. "Hello," she managed belatedly.

"Charlotte? Is that you?"

"Oh, Jonathan—y . . . yes. It's me." I think, she added silently. She'd been dreaming of Sam—again—and imagining that the warm sunlight now falling across her face had been his feathery touch.

"You sound funny," he said suspiciously. "Are you alone?"

Not because I want to be, she thought instantly, focusing groggily on the alarm clock by the bed. "Who else would be here, Jonathan? It's only—my god—it's ten o'clock!"

At last, he seemed to understand, but his voice said he still didn't believe it. "Did I wake you?"

"No, no," she stuttered. "I . . . I was . . . in the shower, that's all. I didn't realize I was running this late." She sat up and ran her fingers through her hair. Across from the bed, in the well-positioned mirror, a harpy with Medusian hair and startled gray eyes stared back.

"You must be getting into that Florida life-style."

From his tone, Charlotte could tell his words were not meant to be a compliment, and she couldn't help but remember what Sam had said last night at the restaurant. Perversely, she echoed his words. "That may not be an altogether bad idea, Jonathan. We could all stand to relax a little occasionally."

"Are you implying something, Charlotte?"

She took a deep breath. "No. I'm merely pointing out that there's more to life than work. I think we've both forgotten that, and Florida has reminded me. Sometimes I wonder if we shouldn't enjoy life more. You know, take some time to smell the flowers, as they say."

"You better forget about the flowers and take care of your career."

Anger rose up like one of the waves outside her window. "What is wrong with you?" she blurted out. "Is work all you ever think about?"

His voice held an injured tone. "My career is very important to me, Charlotte. I thought you felt the same way."

"I do," she argued, "but it's not my entire life. I want . . ."

"What?" he said, filling her pause impatiently. "What *is* it you want, Charlotte? Are you trying to tell me something?"

Yes, she thought with startled surprise, *I think I am*. "I, well, I . . ." Her words drifted off uncertainly as a tiny voice of caution spoke in the back of her mind. Jonathan represented respectability, stability, the family life she'd never had. She'd better be certain of what she was doing, she thought. "I just wanted to let you know about the condos," she finished incongruently. "I toured all the units yesterday. They're in pretty bad shape.'' She paused briefly. ''Why didn't you tell me you knew the property needed work?''

His answer was immediate and sharper than usual, if that was possible. ''I didn't know they did.''

''That's not what Dana Schoen said.''

''And who, pray tell, is Dana Schoen?''

Charlotte gritted her teeth. She hated that snotty tone he used when he didn't know what was going on. ''She's the real estate agent that handles the rentals of the units, Jonathan.''

Jonathan cleared his throat, a dry, parched sound. ''Oh, I'd forgotten her name, but, frankly, I don't recall her saying a thing about the condition of those stupid condos.''

''I saw her yesterday. She told me—''

''Well, if this Schoen woman mentioned it, I forgot.'' The short pause lengthened, and Charlotte could imagine Jonathan tapping the end of his black Mont Blanc pen against his marble desk top. ''If you can't handle this project, Charlotte, I'll send—''

Her stomach tightened at his superior tone. ''I can handle the situation,'' she finally snapped, ''but it might have helped me if I'd known what to expect. I don't like surprises, that's all. The condition of the project caught me short and the tenants, well . . .''

''What's wrong with the tenants?'' he immediately asked, suspicion raising his voice.

Charlotte leaned against the headboard. ''Nothing, they're older people, that's all.''

''Well, that's just great. We need young, upscale types in there, or we're never going to sell those units.'' She heard him take a sip of his coffee then imagined him setting the ivory china cup precisely into the saucer.

"What about this Gibson person, Charlotte. What kind of man is he?"

Explaining Sam Gibson was more than she could handle right now. "I'll tell you later, Jonathan, I really need to get going. Did you need anything else?"

The pause over the wire hummed with suspicion, and Charlotte held her breath. When he finally spoke, she let her breath out slowly, a sigh of relief she didn't fully understand. "No, that's it," he said briskly. "But, Charlotte?"

"Yes?"

"Try and get some work done today, please?"

He was waiting for her answer, but Charlotte had only one—she slammed the receiver down as hard as she could, her sense of satisfaction outweighing any future consequences.

An hour later she pulled into the parking lot at Safe Harbor. Snapping off the engine, Charlotte took a quick look around to reassure herself. Juan was nowhere in sight.

With her notebook and keys in hand, she stepped from the car and headed for the first unit. The lock turned after a few tugs and Charlotte found herself inside the musty condo.

Walking briskly to the opposite end of the den, she mimicked Sam's earlier movements, pulling the draperies aside, then sneezing in the cloud of dust that erupted with the fabric's movement. After a second's hesitation, she threw open the sliding glass door leading down to the beach.

Fresh air poured into the room, and Charlotte sniffed appreciatively. Colorado's air was sharp, definitive, but this soft breeze had a sensual feel that made her want to pull off her jacket and roll up her sleeves. Without a thought, she did just that, hanging the black coat over a chair and thinking again that she'd have to do some shopping. She still needed shoes, and the black gabardine skirt and matching sweater she wore were better suited to a ten o'clock business meeting than her present activities.

Walking slowly through the den and kitchen, Charlotte spent the next hour cataloging every broken spring in the couch, every mark on the walls, every spot on the carpet. The kitchen took the most time. She had to do a complete inventory of the contents, from chipped plates to jelly glasses. By the time she finished, she knew she was going to be in Destin for more than six weeks. More like six months!

The bedroom and bath went quickly. All the linens were in terrible shape, little more than rags, actually. The more she saw, the more she realized just how badly the bank had been cheated. Even when brand new, the units had been furnished shoddily, with the cheapest materials available.

Checking her watch, she walked out into the sunshine. Only five more to go! Maybe Jonathan would think she'd done "some" work, when she called this evening and gave him a report.

Adroitly sidestepping the broken boards on the walk, she made her way to the second unit. She stuck the key in the lock and turned, but nothing happened. Three trys later, her hair sticking to the back of her neck, she began to get angry.

"Jiggle the knob to the right when you turn it. That'll do the trick."

Charlotte turned at the sound of the voice. It belonged to the older woman who'd told her where Sam was the first day Charlotte had arrived. With broad, vigorous strokes she continued to sweep the small square of concrete outside her condo. She was so short the handle of the broom almost topped her head, and as she dragged the bristles back and forth ashes from her cigarette fell to the newly-swept porch.

"Thanks," Charlotte said. "I thought there must be some secret to it."

"Yeah." She stopped and leaned against the faded-blue handle, removing her cigarette from the corner of her mouth. "Everybody has trouble with it."

Charlotte tried once more, but the lock refused to budge. Without saying anything else, the older woman dropped her broomstick and crossed the square of grassy sand separating the two units. "Here," she demanded, "lemme me give it a shot."

Today, she wore a brightly printed housedress splashed with giant red hibiscus and purple orchids. It completely overshadowed her tiny figure. Her gray hair frizzed around her head like a wooly halo and she was barefoot. Standing back, Charlotte watched as the woman crammed her cigarette into the corner of her mouth then grasped the brass knob with two brown-spotted hands. She didn't look big enough—or strong enough—to even turn the doorknob, but after a quick twist and a grunt, she made the door fly open.

"There you go," she said, holding her hand out to indicate the entrance. "It's just kinda ornery sometimes."

"Thanks." Charlotte smiled her appreciation and held out her hand. "I'm Charlotte Huntington."

"Myrtle Francis. Glad to meet you, Charlotte." Her hand felt like a child's, but her grip was as strong as a man's.

She squinted up at Charlotte and pulled on the cigarette, still hanging from the side of her mouth. The ash was about an inch long. "I understand you're here to spiffy this place up."

Charlotte suddenly realized where she'd heard Myrtle's

name. This was the woman Sissy had referred to—the one who'd described Charlotte as that "silly woman from the bank." She kept her smile on. "I'm certainly going to try, Miss Francis."

"Oh, for heaven's sake, call me Myrtle. Miss Francis sounds like a schoolteacher."

In spite of herself, Charlotte smiled again, but this time it was genuine. "All right—Myrtle."

The tiny woman nodded once, then stepped back toward her own condo. She spoke over her shoulder. "If you get too tuckered out, knock on my door and I'll share something cold to drink with you. It's mighty hot to be poking around in those dirty old apartments." With that, Myrtle disappeared into her house, a long trail of cigarette smoke the only clue she'd been there.

By the time Charlotte finished the second condo and was halfway through the third, her black skirt was gray with dust and her makeup had disappeared. Her notebook was almost full and her stomach was completely empty. She decided to stop for lunch.

Just as she started toward her car, the deep rumble of a motorcycle—it sounded like the one she heard late every night, but she wasn't sure—broke into the sticky silence, drowning out even the roar of the surf. Seconds later, an enormous Harley wheeled into the parking lot and drove straight at her. A dusty shower of grit and smoke enveloped her as the driver braked and turned, the chrome dazzling in the sunlight.

Blinking at the muscular figure through tearing eyes, Charlotte watched as he pulled off his black helmet. She should have known.

It was Sam.

FIVE

Her ears throbbed from the dull pulse of the huge engine as she tried in vain to brush off the settling cloud of dust he'd brought with him. Raising her eyes to his, her glare already in place, Charlotte took one look at the man astride the imposing vehicle and slowly drew her breath in.

She couldn't decide which was more impressive—him or the low-slung motorcycle that was cradled between his long, lean legs. He ran a hand through his tangled hair, shook it out and grinned as the engine continued to pulse with a guttural rhythm—a sound she felt as much as she heard. With catlike grace, Sam reached forward and twisted the key.

The black muscle shirt he wore emphasized the width of his upper arms and chest. Tight, black jeans, low on his hips, stretched over his thighs and ended at feet encased in boots. As she stared at him, the palms of her hands turned wet.

"You look a little hot and bothered," he drawled, lowering his sunglasses and looking at her above the rim. "Want to go for a ride and cool down?"

She swallowed hard and tried to pull herself together. "I looked better before you got here," she said, resuming her efforts at brushing herself off.

He threw his leg over the seat and watched her attempts. "I doubt that," he said with a lecherous grin. "You couldn't look much better unless, of course, you had on a little less, like one of those cute string bikinis—"

"*I've* been working," she interrupted stiffly, flustered by his admiration. She tried for a pointed glare toward his motorcycle, but somewhere between her intentions and her actions, the glower came out more like a smile.

"So have I," he replied, his look turning serious. "I've been arranging capital improvements to our little project."

"Capital improvements?" she repeated skeptically.

"Yes. I'm pleased to say that just in time for the annual Fourth of July celebration, Safe Harbor will have a new volleyball net."

Charlotte rolled her eyes. "I'd hardly describe that as a capital improvement."

He stood up and pulled a worn plastic sack from a pack at the rear of the cycle. "Well, you haven't seen the old one," he said, lifting one blond eyebrow at her. "Have you had lunch?"

"No, I was just—"

"Come on," he said, starting toward his condo. "A friend of mine owns a boat, and it just came in. I've got three pounds of fresh shrimp."

Not bothering to wait for her, he threw open his front door and disappeared inside.

Charlotte stared as the door slammed behind him. Did she really want to follow him? Licking her dry lips, she stared down at the diamond sparkling on her finger. Who was it she didn't trust? Him or herself?

"To hell with it," she muttered, starting toward the door. Jonathan was thousands of miles away. And even if he wasn't, why would he care? She had to eat lunch, didn't she?

Lunch! Sam cussed under his breath as he pushed open the door to his condo. What in the hell had gotten into him? He should have known better. She'd probably complain because there wasn't a white linen cloth on the table and sterling silver beside the plate, but somehow the invitation had gotten out before he'd thought about it.

He threw the sack of shrimp into the sink, then tossed his helmet and pack on the couch. They both bounced once and rolled to the corner where Punch opened one eye from his bed. He immediately went back to sleep.

Charlotte's heels clicked against the tile entry, and a second later she entered the kitchen. She looked so good standing there in that short black skirt and tight little sweater, it made his chest hurt. How could one woman look that inviting but be that uptight? Turning, he grabbed a pot from under the stove, filled it with water, dumped in a spice bag and the shrimp, then put it on the back burner.

"Make yourself comfortable," he said with a gesture toward the table and chairs. "How about a beer?"

He opened the refrigerator and hung one arm over the top of the door, staring at her, waiting for her answer.

"I don't drink—"

When he saw her mouth pucker, he remembered. "—beer," he finished for her. She nodded once.

"Iced tea, then?"

"That's fine."

He pulled out a frosted pitcher and set it down on the counter, then got a glass from a nearby cabinet. As he took the ice cubes out of the freezer, he paused and leaned back to stare at her from around the door. Something about Charlotte Huntington brought forth his need to torment.

He held out one cube like a gift. "Would you like this in your glass or down your—"

An instant apricot blush ran from her forehead down, rewarding him for his efforts. "I . . . in the glass will be fine."

He grinned, then tossed the melting ice into her glass, amber tea following it. When he handed it to her, their fingers brushed then sparked together like two loose wires. Sam's eyes locked with hers, the tension so instantly thick he thought it should be visible, something he could cut with his pocketknife. She blinked then pulled the glass toward her, emptying it in one gulp. When she finished, she laid the icy glass against the vee of her neck and closed her eyes, a move he knew she'd made to break his stare—and the tension. It didn't work.

"I can't believe we have so much to do," she said, her eyes downcast. "Those units need everything done to them, and it's going to take us so much longer than I thought. If they'd just been taken care of properly, none of this would be necessary . . ."

Sam watched her mouth, his irritation at her implication competing with his growing fascination. Her lips were so full, so soft looking, so inviting. . . .

His eyes fell to the frosted tumbler at her neckline. From the glass to her skin, a single drop of water had slipped downward where it now glistened like an expensive diamond. For one long minute, the bead of moisture hung then it glided silently down . . . down to the waiting shadows between her breasts. In an instant, Sam was consumed with the need to bend his head to her skin, to taste that single, silent drop—and to taste the rest of her, too.

Without thinking further, he reached out and took the glass from her hand. Her eyelids flew open, revealing grey depths suddenly as stormy as the Gulf in November, but with the instant knowledge of his intent. Setting the glass down with a thud, he pulled her into his arms.

Even though they both recognized the inevitability of his move, she asked the question he knew she would. "What in the hell do you think you're doing?" she said, her hands pressing against his chest.

"I'm kissing you," he replied in a voice hoarse with need. "Something I should have done the first day I saw you."

Tightening his grip on her forearms, Sam pulled her closer, then bent his head to hers. As their lips touched, she opened her mouth to continue her protest, and he seized the chance.

He silenced her with his tongue, the tip probing into the soft center of her mouth, muting any further complaint she might have spoken. Grateful for the instant of stillness, it took Sam a few moments to realize he was savoring more than just the absence of sound.

He could taste the lingering sweetness of the tea she'd just drunk, and her tongue was still cold from the icy drink. Beneath his fingers, her arms were soft and warm— a woman's arms with all the promises they held. He found his hands tightening and without really realizing what he was doing, but understanding only that he had to, he pulled her even closer.

The resistance in her palms weakened, and Sam plunged his tongue further into her mouth. Instantly, without a second's warning, she snaked her arms around his neck and drew him to her.

He might have been surprised had he taken the time to think about her actions. Instead, he reveled in them—and her. High, firm breasts pushed insistently against his chest, demanding his attention while the scent of her perfume rose in a heady mist around them. Pressing her back against the counter, he tore his lips from hers and traced a path of lightning desire down the line of her jaw, nipping at her earlobe as he went.

He had meant only to kiss her, to silence his need to taste her. But instead, somewhere between his intentions and her mouth, Sam lost track of what he was doing, and desire—stronger than he'd ever felt for any woman in his life—hit him like a one-ton bomb. Obviously, judging by the deep murmurs coming from the back of Charlotte's throat, the barrage had claimed more than just one victim.

Sam wrapped his arms around her and lifted her to the kitchen counter, burying his face at the juncture of her breasts, licking that one drop of moisture that had started him on this perilous journey. Wrapping her legs around his waist and her arms around his neck, she clung to him with a strength that astonished him, murmuring his name over and over in a litany of hunger.

Sam knew the kiss was hot—hotter than any he'd ever had before, but when the hiss of rising steam and boiling water reached his ears, he knew he'd gone too far. He jerked his head from her breasts and cursed soundly.

In a daze, Charlotte watched Sam tear himself from her arms and run to the stove. The pot of water and seafood was boiling so hard that pink shrimp were jumping from the beat-up container as if they were still alive and trying to escape. Punch was reaping the bonanza as fast as his short, fat legs could carry him. Sam grabbed the handle of the pot, cursed again, and shook his hand. Reaching for the kitchen towel on the nearby counter, he wrapped it around his fingers and lifted the pot off the burner, placing it on an unlit coil.

Sam looked at her in mock disgust, his chiseled face softened by a grin as he picked up one of the shrimp and threw it to the floor. ''Our lunch is rubber.'' Punch caught it on the second bounce. ''See what you did?''

Horrified, but not by the culinary disaster, Charlotte

jumped down from the counter. "I didn't have anything to do with that—you were cooking."

He started to laugh and took two steps toward her. "I'll say! As a matter of fact, I'd say we were *both* cooking." With a smile that sent her heart pounding, he lowered his voice and spoke again. "What do you say we move on—to dessert? There's always room for—"

"Are you crazy?" Her hand went to her throat. "I thought you wanted lunch, not . . . well . . ."

With eyes that narrowed, he stepped closer, and Charlotte found herself backing up and holding her hands out in front of her. "As I recall," he drawled, "you weren't exactly complaining."

"Y . . . you caught me by surprise."

"Do you always kiss like that when you're surprised?"

Charlotte raised her hand to her lips, but it was too late now. "I don't know what you're talking about," she sputtered.

"Oh, no? Shall I refresh your memory?" He stepped closer.

"Stop it, right there," she warned.

He glared at her a moment longer then threw his hands up in obvious defeat. "Oh, forget it. I've never forced a woman yet. I guess I'm too damn old to start now."

"Thank you," Charlotte said primly. She turned away from him and faced the kitchen counter, pulling at her sweater in her nervousness. Behind her, she heard muffled curses as Sam began to clean up the mess of shrimp and water.

Her knees were as rubbery as the shrimp he'd thrown at Punch, but she'd die before she'd let Sam Gibson know it. Leaning her hands against the cold tile before her, Charlotte closed her eyes and breathed deeply. She didn't know what he called that, but she wouldn't have described it as a kiss. It was more like jumping off a cliff—sailing off into the wind, yet knowing that someone was there to catch you.

Before she could stop herself, Charlotte thought of the last time Jonathan had pecked her cheek. She almost laughed out loud, then brought herself up short. What was more important in a man, for goodness sake—working hard or kissing well? And why, for the love of god, couldn't one man do both?

Her heart was beating so loud she was sure Myrtle could hear it next door, but Charlotte was determined to act cool. If Sam Gibson knew the real effect he had on her, she'd never have a chance. With a casual air of what she thought was sophistication, she turned around to face him, bound and determined to regain control of the situation.

"As I started to explain earlier, I've been examining the bank's condos. The interiors are bad, but the exterior is really going to need some work." She ran nervous fingers through her bangs. "I don't understand why you think—"

With a ravaging grin that told her he knew exactly what she was doing, he stood up and threw the dish towel he'd been using into the sink, obviously deciding to play along with her plan to ignore the kiss. "Why in the hell do you care what I think?"

His question stopped her cold. *Did* she care? She licked lips that were still swollen from his kiss. "I . . . I can't sell my condos with yours looking bad, you know that. I've got to get these units sold or—"

"Or what? You won't get a corner office?"

Surprised at his perception, she stood her ground. "Maybe, but primarily because it's my job," she said grudgingly, "and I'm going to do it. And, I'm going to make you fix yours, too," she promised.

He leaned against the counter and crossed his arms. The

muscles bulged as his eyes sparked with dangerous intent. "Oh, really?"

"Yes." She swallowed hard. "If you don't, I'm going to start on my own and send you the bills." She put her hands on her hips and glared at him. She was trying for menacing, but she had the feeling she wasn't achieving it.

"I'll help." He paused to unfold his arms and hook his thumbs into the belt loops at his waist, his fingers splayed against his hips. His electric eyes glared at her like two blue-hot flames. "When I'm good and ready."

"And when will that be?" she pressed.

"I'm not sure." He nodded toward Punch as he sat in the corner, daintily eating the last of the shrimp. "My 'people' will get in touch with your 'people.' " He raised his eyebrow, one side of his mouth going up in a lopsided grin that went straight to her gut. "We'll 'do' lunch."

"This is serious," she insisted. "I have work to do."

"So do I," he countered. "Very important work."

"Right—like what?"

Sam's face softened, and the effect on Charlotte's insides was drastic. "Living, for one. Taking the time to enjoy life, to savor what you have. Hell, to smell the flowers if you've got to have a damn cliche to understand."

Her face flushed as she remembered using those same words when she'd spoken with Jonathan. Somehow, when Sam said them, though, they took on an entirely new meaning. Defensively, she glared at him, then snatched up her purse and notebook. "I can see this conversation is going nowhere," she said, tucking one loose strand of dark hair behind her ear. "If you suddenly get any sense, I'll be here tomorrow. *Working*!"

By the time Charlotte's angry energy had dissipated, day had given way to night, and the parking lot at Safe

Harbor sat empty and quiet as she locked up the last unit. Sam's motorcycle was nowhere in sight.

She dumped her notebook on the hood of her car, then abruptly turned and headed toward the picnic table. She needed some time and space to think about what had happened today, and an empty hotel room didn't seem the place to do it in.

Before she could consider the situation, however, she caught the biting smell of smoke. Lifting her head, she immediately spotted the red tip of a glowing cigarette. Myrtle was standing two-feet away, puffing furiously on a cigarette and staring at Charlotte through narrowed eyes. "You look like something the cat dragged in. What's wrong?"

Charlotte shook her head but grinned. "Is it that bad?" She held out a hand toward the empty bench. "Why don't you join me?"

"I will if it ain't catchin'." She shuffled nearer, her soft house slippers dragging in the sand. She crammed her cigarette into the corner of her mouth and pulled out the bench. Charlotte rose to help, but the older woman waved her off, accomplishing the task quickly. She sat down with a heavy sigh as Charlotte eased back onto her own bench.

"Damn thing weighs a ton. I told Sam he ought to get us some of that fancy stuff out here, but he hemmed and hawed and said he didn't have no way to get it delivered right now." Leaning her head back, Myrtle took a deep drag on her cigarette. "I swear to God that boy is more than useless sometimes, but I have to admit I love him, damn his ornery hide."

The red tip turned toward Charlotte and glowed brighter for two seconds. A puff of smoke drifted over. "Who in the hell wouldn't, though?" Myrtle continued in a defensive voice. "The man's as good looking as the devil himself, and a real smooth talker to boot. What's not to like?"

Charlotte considered the question while Myrtle went on listing Sam's good points. "He never gets in a snit over the rent, doesn't care if we're a few days late. Fixes things on a pretty regular basis, doesn't mind if we have pets—"

"Wait a minute," Charlotte interrupted. "Back up. Did you say he fixes things promptly?"

The red tip swung back, then moved up and down. "Yup. Every time my toilet plugs up, he comes right over, no problem."

Charlotte pondered the ramifications of this last bit of praise as Myrtle continued.

"Now, I have to admit I've talked to him several times about that danged sidewalk, and he promised he'd get right on it, but so far . . ."

Charlotte glanced backward at the offending boardwalk. The gaping hole where she'd ruined her shoe was an inky spot within the darkness of the night. Somehow it didn't seem to bother her as much as it had before.

Myrtle removed her cigarette and tapped the edge of it against the table, the long ash falling to the sand as she laughed. "I guess, to tell the truth, he could be a little faster on some of the fix-ups around here but, honey, with the rent Sam charges, he can't afford to do much more."

Charlotte couldn't contain her curiosity. "It's low, then?"

Myrtle nodded. "Oh, yeah, the best in town." She ground her cigarette out against the table, then named a figure Charlotte couldn't believe.

"But that's impossible," she said, turning to the tiny, grey-haired woman. "He couldn't even cover his mortgage with rent that low. Are you sure?"

Through the dusk, Myrtle stared at Charlotte as if she'd asked for her last cigarette. "I may be old, but I ain't stupid, sweetie. I know how much rent I pay."

The air was filled with the cry of two pelicans as they flew overhead. Charlotte sat in shocked silence, trying to digest this newest piece of information as Myrtle dug into the voluminous pockets of her housedress. Finally, she found what she was looking for, and her hands reemerged holding a lighter and another cigarette. The flame danced in the evening breeze as she cupped her hand and lit the end of the cigarette.

When Myrtle spoke again, Charlotte felt invisible, as if the older woman was talking more to herself than to Charlotte. "Sam reminds me a lot of my first husband," she said quietly, her voice going soft with remembrances from long ago. "He was such a good man—kind, sweet, generous. Not like some that came after him, that's for sure." She turned her head toward the sound of the waves. "We were married for almost ten years before the war started." She paused, the sound of a jet rumbling in the distance. "He never came back."

"Why does Sam remind you of him?"

"For one, they'd both give you the shirt off their backs—and fine backs they both were, I must say." She grinned slyly through the smoke surrounding them. "I'm sure you've probably noticed that about Sam by now."

Charlotte found herself grinning back, liking the old woman more and more. "Well, he doesn't wear very many clothes. It'd be hard not to notice."

"That's true, that's true." She pulled on the cigarette, and for a moment, Charlotte thought she'd forgotten her story then she started again. "They resemble each other in another way, though; a more important one, I'd say."

"And that is?"

"My husband made me enjoy life. That wasn't always something that was easy to do back then. The country was falling to pieces—the depression, ya know. Why, before we married, I put the groceries on the table by cleaning churches." She shook her head as if dislodging the painful memories. "Point is, Johnny could make me smile, no matter what, and Sam's like that, too. It's a rare gift in a man."

She narrowed her eyes and batted at the smoke as though she wanted a better look at Charlotte. "You look like you could use some smiling, if ya don't mind me saying so. You're too young to have your face all puckered up like that."

For a moment, Charlotte's mouth hung open, her shock at Myrtle's frankness overwhelming, then she burst out laughing, surprising even herself. How could she get mad at a woman who looked like a bird and smoked like a forest fire?

Myrtle's wrinkled face split into a big grin, the tobacco-stained fingers wiggling the cigarette back and forth. "I'm glad you're taking it so well, honey. It's the mark of a good woman to be able to handle honest criticism."

The shared laughter was a release, and the anxiety she'd been holding inside began to ease. She hadn't realized until now how tense and unhappy she'd been lately. She looked down at the diamond and began to twist the stone around her finger.

Myrtle caught the sparkle and grabbed Charlotte's hand, dragging it closer to her eyes for a better look. "Is that an engagement ring?"

"Yes," Charlotte admitted, "it is."

Myrtle dropped her hand and raised her eyes to stare unabashedly at Charlotte. "Now, that's the way you looked when I first walked up. What's the matter, don't ya love him?"

Charlotte grinned in the darkness. "Do you say everything that crosses your mind?"

Myrtle's cigarette glowed like a tiny star across the

table. "Yeah, I do. Life's too damn short when you get to be my age not to say what you mean."

"Well?" the old lady asked after a minute's pause. "What's wrong with him?"

"With who?"

Myrtle nodded impatiently toward Charlotte's hand. "Your husband-to-be. You look like you'd rather discuss interest rates than him."

"I would—they'd be more interesting!" The words popped out before Charlotte knew what she was saying. They exchanged startled stares, then both women burst into laughter again.

"Oh, God," Myrtle gasped, "it's catching. You're going to be as bad as I am before the night's over."

"There're worse things, I suppose," Charlotte countered, her defenses down in the friendly dark. "You obviously enjoy life a lot; I'd certainly rather end up in that situation than in the one I'm thinking about now." She shook her head, her amusement dissolving, her depression returning. "I'm pretty confused, if you want the truth. My dad wasn't around for long, and all my mom would say was to find a man who was respectable." She stared out over the water, the luminescence eerie in the darkness. "I found one that fits her description, but I'm not too sure he fits me."

Myrtle took a deep draw from the cigarette, the ash growing so long it fell into her lap. She took the sides of her dress in both hands and expertly popped it out, scattering the grey embers before they could do any damage.

"Well, I can give you plenty of advice about men, that's for sure. Been married four times," she said proudly.

Charlotte took a deep breath and turned her head toward the drifting smoke, instinctively understanding that Myrtle's concern was genuine. "How do you know if he's the *right* one? I mean, the one you want to spend the rest of your life with?''

"That's easy," Myrtle puffed. "If he's the right one, you're miserable when you're away from him and you're miserable when he's around. You think about him constantly when he's gone, but when he's there you can't breathe good, your heart acts like it's been running a race without the rest of your body along, and you turn blind."

Charlotte laughed. "That sounds more like a disease than love."

"Love is a disease, honey. Don't you know that?" She flicked the cigarette into the sand in front of them, then turned her eyes to Charlotte, her expression serious. "You know he's the right one," she said, "when you think you'll die if you can't be around him. He's the wrong one when you can go for days and not even give him a second thought. The man you really love should be an obsession to you. He'd be like booze to an alcoholic, crack to a druggie." She dug into her pockets and pulled out another package, then continued. "Like cigarettes are to me," she finished with a grin.

Charlotte watched Myrtle repeat the ritual of flame to tip, and thought about the tiny woman's words. Sam was a stranger, a man she'd just met, yet he had such a pull over her that she was scared. The intense need she had to see him, to hear his voice, to watch him walk, sounded just like what Myrtle had described, but that was simply impossible. Charlotte couldn't accept the illogical logic. She couldn't be falling in love with a man she didn't even know. Could she?

Two weeks had passed, and Sam was as scarce as a snowman on the beach.

Everyday Charlotte went to the condos, to polish her plans, to measure rooms, to accept delivery on materials, but Sam was nowhere to be found. She was forced to accept the fact that he was not interested in any of the repairs she'd been overseeing, or apparently in her. As she drove her car back to the hotel, she denied the flare of disappointment inside as this fact registered.

Sam Gibson was the most irritating man she'd ever had the misfortune to meet. He looked like a Hell's Angel and acted like a bum. In addition to that, he took nothing seriously and his innuendos were a constant reminder of her own passionless existence.

He was everything she'd ever dreamed of in a man.

In minutes, she arrived at the hotel, went straight to her room, and peeled off her clothes. A quick shower helped, but her restlessness stayed with her. There was nothing left to do but walk.

She threw on clean clothes, wrapped her hair in a scarf, and ran out the door. Not bothering to wait for the elevator, she clattered down the stairs and headed toward the pool and the boardwalk leading to the beach.

For thirty minutes, she plowed down the beach, the rolling waves to her left, sand dunes and elegant high-rise condos to her right. Walking was the only way she knew to burn off her agitation. Even back home, when the job or Jonathan or a customer got to her, she'd head to the nearest park and walk it off. Usually, it only took ten minutes.

As her feet finally slowed and her breathing returned to normal, Charlotte realized she was heading directly into the most beautiful sunset she'd ever seen. The entire sky had shimmered into a gorgeous shade of apricot, courtesy of a sun no longer visible, and a quiet crowd of people lined the beach to watch the incredible display. On an empty patch of damp sand, surrounded by water, Charlotte drew to a stop.

What was wrong with her?

She turned and moved up the beach to a row of abandoned wooden chairs facing the water. Sinking to the hard slats, she perched and stared at the rolling waves, the evening growing dark around her.

All her life she'd worked hard. The accomplishments had not come easy, the sacrifices had not been empty; high school graduation without a father, college graduation without a sweetheart, now a career but no husband. All she had was a profession—the goal she'd worked toward for years—but having reached it, she found it to be empty. To find herself attracted to a man who didn't value achievement was the ultimate irony.

Reaching down with her left hand, Charlotte scooped up a fistful of sand, then let it trickle through her fingers. *Get a grip. Just because Sam kissed you and showed you a glimpse of heaven doesn't mean you have to have anything else to do with him.* Actually, it'd been more like a peek at hell—heaven would have been if he'd continued.

She stared at the gem on her finger with a heavy heart, the charade she'd been participating in shattering like the light the tiny diamond now dispersed. She couldn't keep it up anymore and look herself in the mirror. She was simply too honest.

Jonathan wasn't the man she loved—he was a safety net. She thought of him as the one thing that was keeping her secure and sane, but in reality, he was tying her up in a trap of her own making—a trap that was growing too tight. He might have been the perfect man for her mother—but he wasn't for her, and it was time that she acknowledged that fact.

Her eyes locked on the engagement ring as the last rays of the sun danced over her hand, catching on the stone and throwing light up to her face. She blinked, then a single teardrop ran down her cheek as she slid off the diamond ring.

* * *

As soon as she returned to her hotel room, Charlotte picked up the phone. There was no reason to wait; she might as well call Jonathan and get it over with.

As if a giant weight had been lifted from her shoulders, she felt a moment's glorious release. But just as immediately, a deep sadness came over her. Jonathan *was* a good man; she just wasn't the right woman for him, and they'd both been foolish to think that she was. Breaking up was the right thing to do, but her hand was shaking when he finally answered the phone.

"Jonathan, we need to talk," she started without any preamble.

"I'm glad you called," he answered in his usual no-nonsense voice. "We *do* need to talk. Have you finished your estimates on the remodeling yet? It's very important that I have those figures by the end of the week—"

"Jonathan," she interrupted, "this isn't about work. It's about us."

She heard his sigh and imagined him putting down his pen. It would lie precisely parallel to the yellow pad he'd been writing on.

"What is it, Charlotte?"

His voice was as cold as the mountain tops he was probably staring at outside his window, and she winced. "I, I . . . well, this isn't exactly easy to say."

He didn't help her, and the long silence over the line was broken only by a faint hum. Finally, she took a deep breath and spoke again. "I've been doing some thinking, Jonathan, and I've decided to return your ring. I . . . I don't think I'm ready for marriage yet." She paused then continued. "I guess I knew this before, and that's why I hadn't been able to set a date. I didn't really understand that until now, though."

When he spoke, his words were like icicles, each one

stabbing her with a stinging sharpness. "You have obviously been harboring some misgivings about our relationship. Why didn't you mention them before?"

"Because I didn't know about them before. I didn't know there was more to life than a balanced spreadsheet."

"And Florida opened your eyes."

She took a deep breath, knowing all the time that it wasn't Florida as much as it was Sam Gibson. She couldn't tell Jonathan that, however, because even if Sam hadn't been there, she knew now Jonathan was not the man she needed. "No," she said simply.

A long pause echoed down the telephone line. "Then what?"

She took another deep breath, but it didn't steady her trembling legs. "I've just come to realize that we aren't a good fit, Jonathan. I don't think I see life like you want me to." She waited then continued, more softly. "You don't see it through my eyes, either."

The pause that followed was even longer and more awkward than the first, but Charlotte didn't know how to break the silence. Miserably, she stared out the window at the rolling Gulf waters. Still he said nothing, and his absolute quiet sparked a flash of anger that she forced herself to ignore. His very calmness was one of the things she'd admired, and now it merely served to strengthen her decision. He was a cold and rigid man, but she'd been blind to that until now.

"Jonathan? Don't you have anything to say?"

"I think you've made a wise decision. If you hadn't said something, I imagine I would have."

Charlotte felt her mouth drop open, shock reverberating down her spine. For a moment, she was speechless, then her surprise took over. "*You* were going to break off with *me*?"

"Yes. I don't mind telling you that you've changed lately, Charlotte."

She opened her mouth to protest, then shut it with a

snap. He was right, she had changed—thank God—but still, he'd stung her pride. She swallowed her surprise. "You're absolutely correct, Jonathan, as usual. Let's leave it at that, shall we?" Before he could say anything else, she spoke again. "I'll mail you the ring. Good night."

To celebrate her new freedom and sense of adventure, the next morning, before she could change her mind, Charlotte stopped at a small dress shop she'd seen earlier. If Sam, and Florida, were going to keep her this hot, she might as well be wearing shorts while she worked.

The bells tinkled over the door as she entered the plush little boutique. Potpourri scented the refreshingly cold air, and her heels sank into deep, mauve carpet as she moved into the center of the shop. From the back a voice called out. "Be right there."

A series of small round tables, covered with ivory lace cloths, held shorts and T-shirts of every color imaginable. Around the perimeter of the room, built-in poles held elegant dresses organized by size.

The cool cotton clothing looked so comfortable that Charlotte had no trouble immediately selecting an armful to try on. Some of the shorts looked a little too short, but from what she'd seen of the women on the beach, anything was fine. If she was going to act like a new woman, she might as well dress like a new woman.

"Charlotte! How nice to see you, again."

Surprised to hear her name, Charlotte looked up at the woman coming from the back of the store. Louise Martin smiled and held out her hands, her huge diamond sparkling in the overhead lights. "Let me take those things and put them in the fitting room for you."

"Louise—you work here?"

She laughed, a silvery, low sound. "You sound surprised. Did you think all I did was play golf?"

Charlotte's face warmed. Actually, that was exactly what she'd thought. "Well . . ."

The older woman laughed again and took the pile of clothing from Charlotte's arms. "That's all Paul would like, but, frankly, I can't stand staying at home all day. I love the man dearly, but sometimes he simply drives me crazy. I bought this little place just so I'd have somewhere to go when he gets too, well, too retired on me."

Charlotte followed her to the back of the shop where she stopped before a curtained alcove. "Did you know men change when they retire?" Louise asked with a grin. "It's been documented."

Louise's bright smile turned Charlotte's lips up, too. "No," she answered, "I wasn't aware of that."

Pulling the curtain back, Louise stepped aside and placed the clothing on a small glass-topped table. "Oh, it's true. They questioned the wives, who were in prison, of course, because their husbands had driven them to a life of crime, and they all said their men had metamorphosed into giant couch potatoes. It was incredible."

Charlotte laughed again and went into the niche, slipping her shoes off. "But Paul doesn't sound that way," she said. "Not if you two play golf all the time."

Louise pulled the curtain back, but left a small gap open, then picked up the first pair of shorts. After undoing the zipper, she handed them in to Charlotte through the break.

"Oh, it wasn't like that at first," she said. "In fact, I thought I'd go nuts at the beginning. That's when I bought the shop, as a matter of fact." She unfolded a T-shirt and passed it through. "Paul worked for an oil company in Houston, and when he retired, we sold everything and moved down here. For six months I thought we'd made the biggest mistake of our lives."

Charlotte pushed the curtain aside and walked to the

nearby three-way mirror. "Oh, that's darling," Louise said. "It fits you perfectly, too."

Turning slowly, Charlotte looked at herself in the mirror. Turquoise shorts stopped right above her knees and the matching pink and turquoise striped T-shirt clung to her curves.

Louise beamed at Charlotte's reflection. "All you need is a little sun on those legs, and you'll be in business."

Charlotte smiled at the compliment, but her mind was still on Louise's last comment. "Why did you think you'd made a mistake?"

The older woman's face turned thoughtful. "Paul had always been an incredibly busy man. He never got home before seven, he traveled constantly, he was just a whirlwind of activity. The minute after we settled in here, he collapsed on the sofa and didn't move for six weeks." She shrugged and raised her eyebrows. "I thought he'd given up. It took me a long time to understand that he was winding down after forty years of constant activity."

"And now?"

She smiled again. "Oh, now he does everything. He golfs, he cooks, he fishes, he plays the stock market. It's just like when he was working, but he's doing things he enjoys. I come up to the shop because he's so busy he makes me tired!"

Charlotte nodded pensively and returned to the dressing room. If Paul had worked forty years and the relaxing time had taken six weeks, maybe Sam's wouldn't last much longer. Surely, he'd get tired of lying on the beach sometime soon.

She tried on five more shorts sets and extravagantly decided on all of them. Then Louise tempted her with a black strapless sundress. The fabric was gorgeous, mainly black but sprinkled with huge grey and blue flowers, managing to appear tropical but very chic at the same time.

"I know you aren't really looking for anything like this, but I think it'd be perfect on you," the older woman said. "Why don't you just slip it on for fun?"

The polished cotton dress was so different from anything Charlotte owned that she couldn't resist, and with a quiet rustle of fabric, she eased it over her head. The strapless bodice dipped low on her breasts, and the skirt was straight and simple, wrapping to one side in a very Dorothy Lamour sort of way.

Charlotte held back the drape and walked outside to look in the mirror. Louise joined her.

"Oh, sweetheart," the older woman breathed. "That looks positively stunning." She stood behind Charlotte and pulled her dark hair to one side, fluffing out her bangs over her forehead. "You look like one of those fabulous stars from an old South Pacific movie."

Charlotte looked at her reflection in the mirror. The dress lightened her eyes to a pale silver color and her skin looked like white satin. In the center of her oval face, her grey eyes gleamed like two burning embers. The rise and fall of her breasts deepened the shadow of her cleavage.

"Don't you think it's a little revealing?" she asked. Her fingers slipped to the top of the neckline and pulled, but the dress refused to cover more.

"Are you kidding?" Louise asked. "I know at least a dozen women who would kill to have a figure like yours. Show it off, for goodness sake."

She was sorely tempted, but even with her new-found sense of freedom, Charlotte wasn't sure she was ready to reveal this much. "I don't know," she murmured. "Where would I wear it?"

"Anywhere you wanted to," Louise answered. "It's a real traffic stopper." She let Charlotte's hair fall back to her neck and stepped to one side as Charlotte moved back into the dressing room.

Still undecided, she slipped out of the dress and picked up her skirt. When Louise spoke again, Charlotte's fingers froze.

"I'd like to see Sam Gibson's eyes if you showed up on his doorstep in that."

Charlotte sucked in her breath, held it for five seconds, then let the air escape slowly. She tried to keep her voice light. "Why on earth would you say that?"

From outside the curtain, Louise spoke. "Well, he's such an attractive man, and the way he was looking at you the other day, I just thought . . ."

"The way he was looking at me?" Charlotte squeaked.

"Yes—when he introduced all of us. At first, I thought he was going to tell us you were his girlfriend, then he said you had some stuff to do. I nearly started laughing until he changed stuff to work. Even after that, though, I have to admit I wondered."

In her shock, Charlotte heard Louise continue to fold her clothing as if she hadn't just dropped a bombshell on Charlotte's emotional front door. "It was very clear from the way he was looking at you, that he'd like to do more than work, that's for sure. Are you going to take the dress, too, my dear?"

Charlotte looked down at the skimpy sundress in her hand, then handed it to Louise, her fingers almost shaking. "Yes. I think I will," she said, taking a deep breath.

She stumbled out of the dressing room, still in a daze, and wrote Louise a check. The older woman continued to chatter, not even noticing Charlotte's distraction, and fifteen minutes later, Charlotte found herself at her hotel.

Despite the kiss they'd shared, Charlotte knew Sam wasn't really interested in her—not in any meaningful way. That was obvious from how he acted; Sam Gibson had fun, not relationships. But maybe Charlotte was ready for that, too. She'd had a relationship with Jonathan; she wanted some fun, now.

SIX

Charlotte had scheduled an appointment with a different contractor—from carpenters, to roofers, to electricians—for every hour. By Wednesday at the very latest, she'd have everyone selected and a time line established.

By Sunday night, only the electrician was left to contact. She cradled the phone against her shoulder and stared at her notebook as she waited for him to answer.

"Yeah?" a gravelly voice finally answered. He'd taken so long that Charlotte had to look down at her list to remember whose number she'd dialed.

"Uh, Mr. Chaney?"

"Who wants to know?"

How pleasant, she thought to herself. "My name is Charlotte Huntington. I'm with the First National Bank of Denver—"

"Where?"

"Denver," she repeated patiently. "Denver, Colorado."

"If this is about Ida Mae, forget it. I ain't paying no more of her debts. That divorce is final—"

Charlotte rolled her eyes, then interrupted, "Mr. Chaney, I'd like to talk to you about a job. This has nothing to do with, uh, Ida Mae. My bank owns six condos down at Safe Harbor, and they need some electrical work.''

"Safe Harbor? Ain't that Sam Gibson's place?''

"Yes,'' she answered. "Mr. Gibson owns part of them; we own the rest.''

"Well, any friend of Sam's is a friend of mine. What'd ya say yore name was, little lady?''

Charlotte ground her jaws together and repeated her name. "Could you meet me tomorrow about six at Safe Harbor? I need a bid.''

"Tomorrow? About six?''

"Yes,'' she answered slowly.

"Well, I don't know . . . might be back, might not.''

Damn! He was the only electrician on the list, she had to talk to him. She made her voice polite. "It's up to you, of course. I'm sure I could find someone else, but it is a considerable job.''

"Cobia's running. I ain't sure how long we'll be out tomorrow.''

Charlotte had no idea who Cobia was, but he apparently ran and was very important to Tom Chaney. Oh, god, she thought suddenly, were there racetracks around here, too? They'd been another favorite haunt of her father's.

Her voice grew frosty. "If you find that more important than money, Mr. Chaney, I'll find someone else.''

"Money's money, honey,'' he answered, chuckling at his rhyming skills. "If I git back, I'll be there. How's that?''

Charlotte hung up the phone, shaking her head in disbelief. What in the world was wrong with these people down here? Didn't any of them believe in earning a living?

Wearing her new turquoise shorts and matching top, Charlotte arrived at Safe Harbor on Monday morning at seven A.M. No one was due until eight, but she wanted to make sure she didn't miss any of the contractors, in case they might stop by early.

She opened up all the units, then settled down to wait on the back porch of the condo at the end, the new sunglasses she'd bought over the weekend perched on the end of her nose. Her fingers reached for her *Wall Street Journal*, but stopped as she raised her face to the morning sun. The rays felt nice with the strong breeze coming off the water, but by ten o'clock even the stiffest wind wouldn't be able to stave off the heat. For the moment, however, Charlotte found herself enjoying the warmth against her pale skin as she pulled in a deep breath of salty air. Overhead, a sea gull cried out, the strident call barely discernible against the gentle roar of the surf.

Forgetting the paper and reaching instead for the plastic cup holding her morning coffee, Charlotte found herself relaxing in a way that was very unusual for her. The sensation was almost uncomfortable. It didn't seem right to be so, well, so comfortable, she thought, pouring the packet of artificial sweetener into the steaming cup. In one word, she felt guilty.

Just as she recognized the emotion for what it was, a deep but not totally unexpected voice broke into her thoughts.

"Well, good morning, Miss Early Bird. What are you doing here?"

She didn't think Sam was a morning person, but there he was—standing at the edge of the porch, loaded down with a cooler, a plastic chair, and a brightly-colored mesh bag.

As though they hadn't shared the most passionate kiss of her life, Charlotte smiled brightly and nodded. A second later, Punch trotted up, a matching plastic bag tied around his neck and dragging in the sand behind him. A fat, pink tongue hung out one side of his slobbery mouth.

She slowly removed her sunglasses and used them to point at Punch. "Not that I care, but it looks like your dog might be choking."

Sam grinned and looked down. "Nah. He's just out of shape. He always carries his own stuff down to the beach. He does get a little winded, though."

Charlotte replaced her sunglasses and nodded as though the spectacle of a dog dragging a beach bag from around his neck was a perfectly normal sight—one she saw every day of her life.

She found herself staring at Sam instead. Today, he wore a bright-blue bathing suit, but it was as skimpy as the black one he'd been wearing the first time she saw him. Maybe it was the kiss they'd shared—the one she was determined to ignore—or maybe it was the way he stood there, his smile lifting one corner of his mouth, his blue eyes drilling her with lazy attention, but something about him simply said SEX.

She reached for the plastic spoon she'd brought and intently stirred her coffee, but her eyes insisted on stealing another look. He'd tamed his wild hair with a blue and white bandanna pulled low across his forehead and knotted in the back. Without the dark curls surrounding his face, his cheekbones looked even higher, his chin even stronger, his mouth even more inviting than before. And those blue eyes—those electric-blue magnets that insisted she meet their head-on gaze—looked even more startling circled by the colored scarf.

"I didn't realize you needed so much paraphernalia for a few hours of sunning," she said.

He grinned and shifted the cooler to his other hand. "We don't just sun for a few hours," he answered in a slow, indolent way. "We take our time and do it right.

All day, if we have to." He licked his lower lip. "Some things take patience, you know."

Charlotte blinked slowly, instantly transferring, in her mind, of course, his insinuation into reality. Images of twisted sheets, gleaming skin, and tangled limbs bombarded her. She knew she should be replying in some fashion but in the face of her imagination, words escaped her.

"Why don't you come with us?"

His whiskey-rough voice played a shiver down her back as she thought about his meaning. He made her too aware of her body. With just his words moving between them, she felt as if a thousand delicious fingers were touching her at once. "I . . . I've got work to do," she finally answered, ducking her head to stare into her coffee cup.

"Work?"

The way he said that one word, insolent with just a touch of disrespect, instantly brought her back to herself. "Yes," she said briskly. "Work. I'm meeting my subs here this morning."

The way she said that one word, work, with such determination and stubbornness, irritated him greatly. At the same time, he couldn't help but grin. She had a lot to learn about sub-contractors and appointments. With a wide smile, Sam set the chair down into the sand beside him, leaning its aluminum frame against his tanned leg. "Which one?"

"All of them," she replied. "The roofer at eight, the plumber at nine, the carpenter at—"

"Whoa, whoa," he said, holding up one hand. "You actually scheduled these people at different times?"

She sat up straighter in the chair, an action which appeared somewhat difficult since it was missing two strategic slats. "Of course. I couldn't have them all coming at once, could I?"

Trying to decide exactly how to say it, Sam removed his sunglasses and rubbed them slowly across the butt of his bathing suit. Squinting, he held them up to the sun and acted as though he were checking his cleaning job. Finally, he placed them on the bridge of his nose and looked at her once more.

She pushed her full, pink lips together and stared at him with a glacial gleam. "You seem to find my appointments amusing."

"No, I don't find them amusing," he answered with a contradictory grin. "What I find amusing is your schedule. What makes you think those people are going to show up?"

She sat very still and stared at him. "Why, I asked them to, of course. And they said they would." She pulled off her own glasses as if seeing better would help her understand. Her forehead wrinkled in confusion and, for a moment, Sam found his distraction starting all over again. When he'd first spied her on the porch, her face tilted up to the sun, her dark hair pulled softly back in a heavy braid, he'd been stopped short. Without her knowing, he'd watched her for a full minute and had enjoyed every second of it.

He let his eyes roam over her once more. Her long, white legs stretched out in front of the table where she sat. She wore turquoise shorts that hugged her slim thighs and a blue and pink striped T-shirt that left nothing for him to imagine. But he did, anyway.

"I don't understand," she said, breaking his train of thought. "Why wouldn't they show up?"

He shook his head and tried to focus on his words. "Oh, they'll show up—but not when you're expecting them."

She arched thin eyebrows and wrinkled her nose. "Is that part of the Florida life-style, too? Like horse racing?"

He tilted his head to one side, his confusion obvious. "There aren't any racetracks in Destin."

"Sure," she answered agreeably. "That's why the electrician couldn't come this afternoon." She twirled her gold-rimmed glasses casually. "Don't try and fool me, Sam. I know Cobia's running this afternoon."

"Cobia!" His mouth dropped, and this time he didn't bother to stifle the loud guffaw that escaped. "Cobia are fish, for god's sake."

Her glasses slipped through her fingers and bounced to the floor. With a muttered oath, she bent over and picked them up. "Of course," she said tightly after she straightened up. "I knew that."

Shaking his head, he continued to grin, then picked up his things. "Punch and I will be at our office, it you need us." He took two steps then stopped and turned. "Watch out for those wild Cobia. Wouldn't want one to run you down." Snickering, he continued down the path.

Well, great, she thought with a frown. That was about the stupidest thing she'd ever said, and Sam Gibson would never let her forget it, either. She quickly crammed her glasses back on her face and picked up the newspaper, shaking it vigorously, as if she had Sam's neck between her hands instead of the stock-market pages.

Two hours later, she'd read the entire paper—twice—and the only sub to show up was the landscaper, the very last man she'd need on the job. Just to make sure she didn't accidentally miss anyone else, she'd attached a note to the front door of the unit where she sat. But no one else showed up.

By lunchtime, she was getting angry.

She headed for the beach. Sam was still sitting down there on his tight little butt doing absolutely nothing to help. Gritting her teeth, she approached him, intent on asking to use his phone to call the cretin subs who apparently couldn't tell time.

He was stretched out in the powder-white sand, looking just as comfortable as the first day she'd found him, only this time he had reading material spread around him— magazines with names like *Cycle* and *Easy Rider*. Somehow she wasn't surprised. She stopped beside his umbrella, and he looked up at her.

"Charlotte!" he said in a pleasant voice. "How goes it?" Before she could answer, he pulled his sunglasses down on his nose and stared at her. "You look a little upset. You better sit down in my shade, or I may end up taking off some of your clothes again."

Charlotte felt her eyes go wide, and she threw a quick glance around to see if anyone had heard. The beach was crowded, but the roar of the emerald water had covered his teasing words. She sat down, as much to shut him up as anything.

Hating to admit defeat as well as to ask him for a favor, Charlotte glared. "None of those idiot construction people have shown up," she said tightly. "I came down here to ask you if I could borrow your phone instead of returning to the hotel."

"Help yourself," he replied, pushing his glasses back up his nose and returning to his magazine. She'd expected some smart-aleck comment, but he simply nodded toward the condos behind them. "Door's open."

"You don't lock your house?"

He stared at her above the magazine and grinned. "Nah. If I locked mine, then Punch would want to lock his, and he'd never keep track of the key."

Charlotte looked around suspiciously. "Is he up there, now?"

Behind the dark glasses, Sam cut his eyes toward her.

"Scared?" he grinned. "He *is* a pretty vicious dog, I have to admit."

"Hardly," she answered. "He's more likely to lick me to death than bite me."

Sam's eyes locked with hers. "Maybe he thinks you taste good."

"You ought to know. You practically had me for lunch the other day."

His lips curled up in a wicked grin. "Oh, no, sweetheart. I'd consider that just an appetizer. A whole meal would be—"

"I . . . I think I'll go use the phone," she interrupted.

"What's your hurry?" he drawled. "Let's have *lunch*, then you can call. You won't be able to reach any of them at noon, anyway."

She hesitated, not exactly sure what kind of *lunch* he had in mind. Was she going to be the main course? The image that flashed into her mind was accompanied by a hot, liquid feeling deep in the pit of her stomach. But before she could reply, he spoke again. "This is a public beach, you're safe."

"I wasn't worried," she shot back.

He tossed his magazine to one side and pulled the cooler toward him. Reaching inside, he lifted out two plastic bags. "I've got shrimp or crab. Which do you want?"

Charlotte had never eaten a crab in her life. The hard shell looked impenetrable. "I'll take the shrimp," she said.

He tossed her the bag of pink boiled shrimp, then reached back into the cooler and took out two beers. Before she could say anything, he popped the top and handed it to her.

"I know, I know," he said before she could speak. "You don't drink beer. Too bad, 'cause that's all I've got."

The sun had shifted and the bright rays were hitting the back of her exposed neck. A trickle of sweat ran down the valley of her breasts, and suddenly the thought of something cold—anything—was very appealing. Charlotte took a second look at the icy can he'd stuck in her hand, then shrugged her shoulders. Why not? Jonathan had always said beer was for people who had no taste—she might as well give it a try since she no longer gave a damn what he thought.

As if she'd telegraphed her thoughts, Sam glanced over at her, his casual air more casual than ever. He lifted one eyebrow and tilted his head toward her hand. "Where's your ring?"

Somehow, she wasn't surprised that he noticed. He might act offhand, but in reality, Sam Gibson missed nothing. "I mailed it back a few days ago," she answered. "I . . . I thought it best to call off the engagement. Things have changed, well, actually, *I've* changed, and I thought it best." She smiled, and shrugged her shoulders. "If you want to know the truth, I think I just barely beat him to it."

Unexpectedly, he made no comment, turning instead to the mesh bag at his feet.

She took a long gulp and watched as Sam pulled out a pair of pliers. The bitter coldness ran down her parched throat with surprising smoothness, and she took another deep swallow.

"I've never seen anyone use pliers as an eating utensil," she commented, indicating the tool with a nod of her head.

"Then you've obviously never eaten crab," Sam replied.

She took another draught from the beer then hiccuped discreetly. "I beg your pardon," she said primly. "But, I've eaten lobster—it's the same thing, just bigger."

"No," he shook his head. "Eating lobster tail in a

fancy restaurant where somebody in a monkey suit pulls the meat out for you is definitely *not* the same thing.''

Charlotte took another drink from the beer, then set the can down and opened her bag of shrimp. ''Frankly, I don't see the diff . . .'' Her words died off as her fingers touched the cold crustaceans. She jerked her hand out of the bag.

''What's wrong?'' he said, looking up from his crab.

She looked up. ''They're still in their shells.''

''So?''

''I . . .uh, I . . .''

He paused and looked at her in surprise. ''Don't tell me you've never peeled shrimp before?''

''Well, of course, I have,'' she lied. ''It's just that I don't care for it, that's all.''

''You don't care for it?'' he repeated slowly. ''Well, now, that's too bad, because you chose shrimp and I got the crab. If you want to switch, it's too late.''

''N . . . no,'' she replied. ''I'll do it.'' Taking another swallow of beer then closing her eyes, Charlotte stuck her hand in the bag and pulled one shrimp out. She opened her eyes, then using her fingernail she started at the tail, managing to dislodge one small sliver of the hard, clear shell.

Beside her, Sam had stopped, his bright-blue eyes crinkling with disbelief behind his glasses. ''Give that here,'' he finally said, grabbing the shrimp from her fingers. ''You'll starve at that rate.''

With a quickness that astonished her, he pulled the legs from the shrimp, then separated the body from the shell in one fluid movement. His hands were fast, almost as fast as they'd been the other day in his apartment. If she'd let him, she thought to herself with a giggle, he would have had her clothes off as easily as he shelled the shrimp.

Reaching into the bag, he rapidly peeled a dozen more then looked up at her. "Got it?" he asked.

She blinked twice then nodded. "Could I have another beer?"

He grinned and reached into the cooler behind him. "Pretty hot, huh?"

She nodded and pushed the slipping sunglasses back up her nose, concentrating on the pile of shrimp still in the bag. It might take her all day, but she'd peel those suckers, by God.

Leaning back against the chair, Sam stared at her as she continued to work. In the growing heat, her shirt was plastered to her breasts and a few wild strands of dark hair had escaped from the braid at her neck.

He'd never met a woman so determined to prove a point, he thought idly, whether it was remodeling a condo or peeling shrimp. He'd been right the first time he'd laid eyes on her. She *was* trouble.

In more ways than one, he continued silently. That much had been very obvious in his kitchen the other day. Charlotte Huntington was just like that pot of shrimp he'd been cooking. Judging from the way she'd wrapped her arms and legs around him, he'd be willing to bet money that she was going to bubble over soon, too. He decided he'd like to be there when it happened.

He returned to the crabs, his concentration broken. Somewhere under that prim exterior, and not too far under at that, beat a heart and a passion that had been pushed back for far too long. He'd like to be the one to turn up the heat, the one to be close by when those feelings finally came to the surface.

He glanced at her from behind his glasses. In her fierce concentration, she'd pulled that luscious bottom lip in between her teeth. As he watched, however, she pushed it back out, the tip of her tongue following it to run over her upper lip. A bead of sweat broke out on Sam's brow.

She took another sip of her beer and blew at her bangs. "God, it's hot," she murmured. "I can't believe it's this hot." Another long pull on the can, and she looked at him above the rim.

"Are you going to eat," he finally asked, "or just peel those damn things?"

Like two pools of liquid silver, her eyes grew large as she glanced down at the growing pile of shrimp, then back up at him. "Well, I have to peel them all before I can start to eat." She spoke patiently as if explaining something simple to a backward child.

"Whose rule is that?" he asked.

"It's the only logical way to do it."

"Maybe, but is it the *only* way to do it?"

She frowned, then took another sip from her beer. "I guess not," she said, her face clearing with a devastating smile. "I *could* eat as I go, couldn't I?"

Without thinking, he reached over and tucked a strand of hair behind her ear, dazzled by the transformation the smile made on her face. She looked as if she were about eighteen and didn't have a care in the world.

"Sure you can, babe," he answered with a grin. "This is Florida. You can do whatever turns you on."

She popped a whole shrimp in her mouth and smiled again, closing her eyes. "Mmmm," she said, opening her eyes once more. "This is great. How's yours?"

Without even realizing what he'd been doing, Sam had cracked over a dozen of the hard-shelled crabs. He looked down at the pile of claws and selected one of the fatter specimens, holding it out to her. "Here. Taste for yourself."

She reached out for the crab claw, but he pulled it back. "Come and get it," he said in a low, steady voice.

Without a word, she leaned over and grabbed his hand, pulling it closer. Her eyes never leaving his, she slowly guided his fingers toward her mouth.

Closing her lips over the fleshy white morsel, she bit down, then slowly tilted her head back until she'd taken all the meat from the claw. With slow, even chews, she ate, her eyes still fixed on his.

Sam's heart began to pound with a rhythm he hadn't felt in a very long time. Even the kiss they'd shared in his kitchen hadn't held the eroticism this did. Fascinated, Sam stared at her mouth.

When she pulled his hand back toward her and nipped at the remaining slivers of meat along the claw, her sharp teeth white in the blazing sun, Sam couldn't stop the game. With her fingers clasped around his wrist, he drew the claw back. Her eyes widened in surprise. Turning his hand slowly until his fingers replaced the fleshy meat, Sam teased her with his touch, daring her further. At the last second, he substituted his fingers for the crab claw and like a cat licking its fur in the sunshine, her tongue lathed his skin with a surprisingly warm wetness. From the equally hot look in her eyes, he knew she was feeling the warmth somewhere else, too.

His breath caught deep in his chest. For the first time since she'd met him, Charlotte's actions were matching her appearance. She had a raw, blistering appetite for more than she knew how to ask for. And now that she'd released that natural craving, Sam felt a matching hunger growing in his own body.

Denying his feelings, Sam pulled his hand away. For one brief second, he'd seen, though. He'd seen what she *could* be, and her passion was just as he had imagined.

She bent her head and picked up one of his paper towels to use as a napkin. Carefully dabbing her lips, she spoke with a prim sobriety. "Thank you. I must get back now."

In a fluid movement that defied any notion of drunkenness, she rose to her feet. "You serve an excellent luncheon," she said with a perfectly straight smile. "I might return to eat at this establishment again." Without a backward glance, she pivoted in the sand and headed back to the condos. With a heavy sigh, Sam turned his eyes back to the emerald water, his desire as uncontrollable as the waves now pounding the shore.

Charlotte stopped by the empty condo, picked up her notebook, then walked directly to Sam's unit, intent on using the phone, then getting out as soon as possible. That man was trouble! Every time she got around him, strange things happened.

Like lunch. She'd never in her life taken food from a man's hand like that—much less licked his fingers afterwards—even if he had stuck them in her face. Sam reached inside of her and yanked out her most primitive behavior, whether it was anger or something else—something she didn't want to even consider.

She marched to his back porch and pulled open the screen door, stepping inside with some reluctance. Going into Sam's home without him there seemed like an awfully intimate thing to do, but she couldn't drive back to the hotel—she might miss someone while she was gone, not to mention the slight buzz the beer had given her.

The overhead fan was twirling lazily, and the cool air washed over her like a blessing. The dim interior of his house beckoned.

She glanced down at the couch where she'd lain and instantly images of Sam and his ice cubes came to her mind, making her heart stumble in remembrance. Pausing by the open door that led into the rest of the house, Charlotte closed her eyes. How would it have felt if he'd continued? If his tongue had followed the watery path the ice had taken first?

With a start that took away her breath, Charlotte realized she'd like to find out. Oh, he was irritating, all right, but that irritation was beginning to rub her in a way that felt pretty good.

She opened her eyes, stared at the couch again, then fled into the interior of the condo as though she could escape her fantasies in there.

Charlotte paused in the center of the room. In one corner, a huge basket of magazines, arranged by size, waited beside an easy chair. Opposite the chair was a beautiful armoire, its tall doors apparently hiding a television and stereo, judging from the wires coming out the back. A small sofa, covered in a print that matched the chair, was centered against the other wall. Two end tables, each with a lamp and an ashtray, rested at both ends of the couch.

There wasn't a phone in sight.

She turned and forced her feet down the hall toward Sam's bedroom. Holding her notebook against her chest as though it could protect her—from what, she didn't know—she stared at the king-size bed. It stretched from one side of the room to the other, or so it seemed to Charlotte. A dark-blue spread, just the color of Sam's eyes when he got really angry, covered the wide expanse. In one corner of the room, a matching recliner sat while a small chest of drawers rested against the opposite wall. The fourth wall was an all-glass patio door.

Outside the door, a small wooden deck extended for about ten feet. At one end, shielded by a wooden lattice, a cedar hot tub bubbled invitingly, the sound of gurgling water a soft counterpoint to the roar of the waves on the beach.

It didn't take much imagination to visualize Sam sitting in that hot tub, steaming water up to his chin, a cold beer in his hand. He would smile that sexy smile—the one that lifted his lips just so and made the lines around his mouth even deeper—and hold out one hand.

She walked around the edge of the bed and sat down abruptly, dropping her notebook to the floor and imagining what it would be like to share that small space with Sam. With very little effort, she knew more than just the water would be hot.

The clean smell of his aftershave enveloped her in a haze of desire, and she let the images run wild in her mind. Sam and her on the deck. Sam and she in the hot tub. Sam and her in the bed. Her thoughts turned more and more explicit until her cheeks were flaming and the blood was pounding in her ears. What was happening to her, for heaven's sake? No matter how attracted to him she was, Sam Gibson should be the last man on this earth she'd really consider having a relationship with, so why was she even thinking about it?

She'd only come in here to use the phone, and now she was sitting on Sam's bed, wondering how it would feel to be crushed beneath his weight and held captive by his hands.

As if flames had suddenly shot out from the mattress, Charlotte vaulted up, horrified that she'd even sat down in the first place. As she moved around the bed, she accidently kicked a small box that had been tucked halfway beneath the frame. To Charlotte's dismay, the contents scattered in the deep pile.

Instantly dropping to her knees, she hurriedly bent to retrieve the bits and pieces, but as she realized what she held, her hands stilled and her heart slowed.

The precious flotsam of Sam's life—faded newspaper articles, dark snapshots, tarnished medals, even a small gold locket—were jumbled together in her shaking hands. She glanced over her shoulder as though she were afraid that he might enter the room at any moment and catch her. She felt like a thief, only she was stealing his memories, not his silver. Slowly, carefully, she separated each cherished article from the other and smoothed the wrinkled papers.

She righted the box and flipped open the lid, fully intending to return everything immediately. Her fingers stopped once more, however. She told herself she shouldn't, but the temptation was too much, and she flipped open the largest item, a double picture frame.

A photograph was on one side and a letter on the other—a letter on presidential stationery. Her eyes widened at the signature on the bottom, but grew even larger as she took in the photograph.

Frozen for the camera, Sam stood regimental straight, the chest of his uniform covered with medals. She recognized only his eyes; the rest of him was so stiff, so different from the man she'd just left that her breath caught in her throat. The knife-edged creases of his pants looked razor sharp, and the hat he wore covered neatly trimmed short hair. There was no hint of his favorite bandanna, his cut-offs, the inevitable beer can.

In a small whoosh, Charlotte exhaled, forcing her eyes to leave his dignified portrait and skim the letter on the other side.

When she finished, she was holding her breath again.

He'd gone beyond the call of duty, it said, shown bravery outside the realm of ordinary men. Her eyes flickered back to his photograph, then to the carpet where the medals that had decorated his chest that day now adorned the floor. She carefully closed the picture frame and returned it to the box, her shaking fingers reaching next for the shiny, beribboned badges.

The cold pieces of metal bit into her warm palm as Charlotte studied the various awards. She didn't know what each one meant; her father had never come home with these kinds of mementoes. It was obvious, however, that Sam had experienced a very successful career.

She swallowed past a tight throat, the realities of his life squeezing out her assumptions. Awards like these were only given to the best.

Dropping the medals back into the box, Charlotte picked up the locket, turning it in the light. The front was engraved with the letter J. With a quick flick of her nail, she released the latch and flipped the golden frame open.

It was empty.

Had he given it to someone, only to have it returned? Had it belonged to some long-forgotten relative? Maybe even his mother? It joined the other items in the box, then she gently closed the lid. With a prayer that she was placing the box back into the right spot, Charlotte slid it halfway under the mattress and stood up.

Sam Gibson wasn't the man he seemed. But then again, she thought with a sigh, who was?

SEVEN

The plumber finally arrived, only an hour and a half later than he'd promised.

No one else came, however, and Charlotte wasn't about to return to Sam's condo to use the phone. All she could do was wait a little longer, but the electrician never showed up. The Cobia must have been plentiful, she finally decided, as she drove back to the hotel.

After taking a quick shower, she slipped into a robe, ordered dinner from room service, and retrieved her copy of the deed restrictions from her briefcase near the front door. She sat down on the balcony outside and began to read. In the same way of all urban areas, any remodeling had to pass a strict code. Charlotte had no desire to get in trouble with city hall; she had her hands full with Sam Gibson.

With a frown of determination, she squirmed against the chair, the cool breeze lifting the lacy collar of her robe as she flipped through the heavy sheaf of papers to find the right spot. She read the first line six times and didn't understand a word. Finally, she cursed and threw them down on the glass-topped table, standing with a grunt of disgust. It wasn't going to work.

She couldn't concentrate, and there was only one man to thank for that.

Moving to the railing, Charlotte stared out over the peaceful scene. Only a faint light remained, bathing the ocean and sand into a pearly opalescence while overhead a huge pink cloud hung, waiting and watching. The wind had died down and a silent, expectant stillness had settled in. The only movement on the entire beach was at the water's edge where a flock of tiny sandpipers rushed back and forth like harried office workers trying to get in the last elevator down. They cried continually in their frantic haste.

Mesmerized, Charlotte stared. Was her life like that?

Sam never seemed to hurry, and he was perfectly happy. So happy, in fact, he felt the need to do absolutely nothing. She tightened her arms across her chest. Obviously, he'd already accomplished his goals, she argued with herself, remembering the box of medals. She'd seen the proof, even if he hadn't said anything.

Tucking her hair behind her ears, Charlotte lifted her face to catch a restless breeze. Overhead, the diamond brilliance of a thousand stars sparkled against the velvet night. She leaned her elbows on the metal railing and stared out at the gentle waves. Why did she notice things here that she didn't at home? Surely there were birds there, but were any of them as exotic as the three huge pelicans that just cruised by in strict formation? Colorado had beautiful lakes, all over the state. Why didn't any of them hold the fascination this emerald water did? And surely there were men in Denver just as virile and sexy as Sam Gibson. Why hadn't any of them caught her eye?

She held her breath and pondered this last question. Wasn't that the crux of the matter? SamGibson. She ran the words together in her mind and wondered what it would be like to lie in his arms on the beach with only the stars and the pelicans to see.

Suddenly, the tranquil night was shattered with an ear-piercing siren. Charlotte jumped back from the railing, her thoughts and her questions scattering like the sandpipers who'd taken instant leave of the beach. With her heart in her throat, she glanced frantically around as the siren continued to blare. In an instant that stretched to eternity, she finally realized what it was—a fire alarm—and it was inside the hotel!

Galvanized into action, she ran back inside her room to the door and threw it open without thinking. Up and down the hall, frantic guests in various stages of undress had done the same. When the metallic speaker at the end of the carpeted expanse began to crackle, they all grew quiet and craned their necks, as if by looking at the small metal box on the wall, they could control the moment.

"This is the hotel security chief. Please proceed to the nearest exit with all possible speed and caution. A fire has broken out—"

Pandemonium took over as the dreaded words sank in, and Charlotte sensed a moment of panic. What to do? Which way to go? With her heart twisting in her chest, she jumped back inside and grabbed her briefcase. With her other hand, she seized the sack of clothing she'd purchased from Louise. Adrenalin fueled her feet as she ran back to the door and joined the stream of terrified guests heading toward the stairwell. The loudspeaker continued to urge them on.

With her pulse pounding in fear, she was pushed and pulled down the hall, helpless to do anything but go where the mob took her. Pressed along the narrow passageway, a moment's hysteria flashed over her as the crowd swarmed in around her. She swallowed her anxiety and forced herself to concentrate on getting out, the copper taste of fear strong in her mouth. As she entered the concrete stairwell, metal stairs biting into her bare feet, the shrill cries of scared children and fearful adults rang in her ears. Like a herd of startled deer, the crowd paused as the acrid smell of smoke reached them, then instantly surged forward with renewed ferocity.

Charlotte's fear rose another notch. She was trapped by the fire behind her and the crush of people surrounding her. Panic seized her breath as surely as the mob held her. She wanted to cry out, to make them slow down, but it was useless. They would listen to nothing except their fear, and even if they had, she knew a second later that there *was* no going back. Her hand brushed out against the rough cement wall of the stairwell—it was already hot! Terror gripped her.

Stumbling down the stairs, Charlotte fought to regain control over her fear, but it was impossible. The crying, screaming, moving mass of people wouldn't let her. As a woman pushed her into the suitcase of the man in front of her, Charlotte cried out. She couldn't tell which was more terrifying—the crowd or the fire.

Her room had only been on the fourth floor, but the stairs seemed to go on forever. Like a record being played on a slower speed, the images and sounds slowed and blurred until Charlotte thought she'd die. The smell of smoke was growing thicker, and her eyes began to tear— from the smoke, she told herself, and not the fear that was threatening to overcome her.

At last, the column of people, shaking with fear, spilled onto the sidewalk of the hotel. Scattering like crazed animals released from a cage, they poured out across the black-topped lot, feeling their way around cars, staring with horror at the fire trucks just rounding the driveway. Stumbling to the grass at the edge of the asphalt, Charlotte sank to her knees, clutching her briefcase and bag of clothes, numb disbelief forcing her mouth open. The faces around her were paralyzed with grotesque fright, frozen in the red strobe lights of the arriving fire engines.

In the amber light of the overhead lamp, she automatically lifted her shaking arm and glanced down at her watch. Only five minutes had passed since she'd heard the first alarm. It felt like five years. Her heart continued to race, the adrenalin rush giving way to a weakness that made her grateful she was sitting.

People continued to stream from the hotel until the parking lot was full of women in housecoats, clutching purses and children, and men looking dazed. Once on the ground, they all followed the same pattern; huddling in small groups, their arms locked around each other, inevitably turning to stare with horror at the flames now shooting out the upper-floor windows. From her seat on the curb, Charlotte did the same, the realization sinking in that flames were dancing where she'd been only minutes before. She took a deep, frightened breath then coughed in the cool, smoky air, her relief finally eclipsing her panic.

The firemen continued to battle the blaze, their long hoses snaking across the parking lot, their yellow slickers taking on strange colors under the vapor lights, but it was obviously hopeless. Flames now consumed the entire west wing of the hotel. Dashing between the huddled groups of evacuees were hotel employees distributing blankets and checking off names. Thankfully, the only casualty so far seemed to be the guests' pride as they realized how they were dressed.

Charlotte pulled in a second, deep breath and tried not to stare at the couple directly in front of her. It didn't really look that strange to see a woman in a man's pajama top, but he looked pretty weird wearing her nightgown.

Charlotte forced down the hysterical giggle that hovered in the back of her throat.

In two hours the blaze was out, but the hotel and parking lot looked like something in Beirut. Broken glass littered the sidewalk, crunching beneath the firemen's boots. Overhead, in the shell that was left, wet and blackened drapes billowed out of shattered windows. The material flapped anxiously in the drafts now chasing through the ruined rooms, lending a ghostly air and sound to the ruined sight. The smokey pall that hung over everything tasted oily on Charlotte's tongue.

The staff of the hotel had rounded up a coffee pot and was dispensing the strong brew as fast as they could. A woman wearing an apron that read *The Donut Hole* stepped gingerly between the fire hoses and splintered glass, offering donuts from a huge white box. Gratefully, Charlotte accepted one, then sat back down on the curb with her coffee. Her knees were still shaky as she turned to listen to the hotel manager. He stood on the back of a pickup and spoke into a bullhorn.

"May I have your attention, please?" He ran a desperate hand through grey-spiked hair and looked at the still-milling crowd. His once-white shirt, now smudged with black and dingy with soot, hung half way out of his pants. A long rip ran down one sleeve. "Please, may I have your attention?" he repeated.

The talk rumbled into an expectant silence. "My staff and I have been trying to find rooms for all of you, but we've run into some difficulties. The Shriners are in town and they have almost every room available. Another group has everything else." The silence erupted into angry rumblings, but he continued, one hand in the air.

"If you will approach the table I've set up, we'll do everything we can to help you out. Please be patient, this make take a while." Dropping the bullhorn to his side and clambering down, he was immediately engulfed by exhausted and confused guests. Charlotte drained the last of her coffee and shook her head. It'd be hours before anything would be resolved.

"Well, I don't care how much it costs," an angry voice hissed beside her. Charlotte turned and looked at the woman wearing her friend's pajamas. She was speaking to the man wearing her pink top.

"If we'd stayed at that place I wanted to, none of this would have happened." She pointed toward the mob by the impromptu registration desk. "I'm not waiting for that to clear out. Call us a cab. We'll find something on our own." The man beside her nodded dumbly, too overcome by the situation to do more than follow her orders.

Charlotte stared a minute longer, then rose. The woman was right—it would be morning before the harried clerks could help everyone. She cinched her silk robe tighter and picked up her scuffed briefcase and ripped plastic bag. There was only one place she could go.

The socket wrench gave way unexpectedly and Sam's knuckles scraped painfully across the rear damper, leaving a trail of blood. His curse beat the drops to the floor.

He was getting tired; he should have quit hours ago, but it was soothing to sit outside and tinker with his Harley this late at night. Usually soothing, he amended, sucking on his bleeding knuckle and flipping off the spotlight he'd trained on the cycle. Tonight, for some reason, the image of Charlotte Huntington's dark hair and silver eyes continued to distract him. He cussed again.

From his vantage point near Sam's outstretched leg, Punch wagged his tail at the blistering profanity and gave a sharp little bark.

Sam looked at the disheveled dog. "That wasn't your name, you dumb son-of-a—"

The sudden brightness of a car's headlights cut a path across the parking lot and halted Sam's words. Ducking his head, he lifted one hand to shield his eyes from the blinding light. He heard a car door slam then, a moment later, a pair of dirty, smudged feet, the toenails painted a delicate shade of coral, appeared beside his leg.

"Can you loan me five dollars to pay for the taxi?"

Sam's eyes slowly traveled the long path from the tips of those incredibly feminine feet, up legs that didn't quit, to the hem of a short, silk robe that barely stopped in time. When he got to her neck, he was grinning widely.

He had no idea why Charlotte Huntington was on his doorstep at one A.M., wearing a bathrobe and carrying her briefcase, but he was sure it would be interesting to find out. She repeated her question.

"Could I *please* borrow five dollars?"

As if he were giving the request some thought, Sam leaned over and looked past her to the cabbie. He'd pushed his yellow cap back on his head to better watch the proceedings. A chewed-off toothpick hung from one corner of his mouth. Sam looked back at Charlotte.

"Five bucks, huh?" He let his eyes drift over her body as he ran a hand thoughtfully up his throat to his rough, stubbled chin. "I'm not sure. We might work out a deal, though. . . ."

The eloquence of her curse surprised him, and with another haughty look, she stepped over Sam and headed toward his front porch. Grinning, Sam jumped up then walked over to the cabbie and stuck the money in the window. "Have a nice night," Sam said with some distraction, Charlotte foremost on his mind.

"Yeah, sure, mister. You, too—if it's possible with that woman." He threw Sam a sympathetic stare, put the car in gear, and took off.

Sam turned and headed back to the porch where Char-

lotte sat in an old chair of Myrtle's. A plastic bag and a
battered briefcase were on the floor beside her. With
slightly crossed eyes, Punch stared adoringly at her, his
nose draped over her bare feet.

She'd slumped against the back of the chair, but as soon
as she saw Sam, she straightened her spine and laced her
fingers together in her lap. "I'm sorry I had to bother
you, but there was a minor problem at the hotel."

Sam sank to the concrete and leaned against the low brick
wall that fronted it, staring at Charlotte. Under the amber
light of the street lamp, he now saw that the paleness of her
skin was not her usual ivory hue; this was a bloodless pallor
that made his heart stand still. A black smudge streaked
down one cheek and her hair hung around her face like a
dark curtain. He wanted to jump up and wrap his arms
around her, but he forced himself to remain calm.

She reached up and pushed at her bangs, the wide
sleeves of the robe falling open. A flash of white underarm
distracted him for a second, then he spoke with an off-
handedness he didn't really feel. "From the looks of you,
I'd say it was more than minor."

Her eyes were two gray embers. "My hotel burned
down." She pointed to the briefcase and plastic bag, her
voice holding the flatness of shock. "That's all that's left.
My purse, my money, even the keys to my rental car—
all gone."

As the seriousness of her words soaked in, a sliver
of fear stabbed Sam's gut. "My God! Did everyone get
out?"

She nodded wearily, then shivered involuntarily. "Yes,
but it w . . . was pretty scary." With a trembling hand,
she pushed her hair back from her face, and Sam felt his
world turn upside down.

What would he have done if something had happened
to her? He instantly pulled back from the thought, but the

realization that he really cared for her kept coming—kept coming, then hit him like a bad spill off his Harley.

She shifted on the hard chair, a flicker of something that looked like pain crossing her face.

"What's wrong?" he immediately asked.

A fierce red blush started at her roots and worked its way down her pale face, her shock giving way to embarrassment. Sam found himself grateful for the hint of color it put back in her cheeks.

"Come on, Charlotte." He tried to soften his voice, coaxing her as best he could. "What's wrong?"

"I . . . I fell down when I was getting in the taxi," she admitted. "I wasn't watching what I was doing, I guess. I was pretty shook up." She bit her lip and looked back up at him. "I think I might have scraped myself pretty bad."

"Think?" he repeated, confused. "Don't you know?"

She shook her head, her dark hair fanning her cheeks like chocolate-colored silk. "It stings, but I can't tell," she finally said, pointing in a vague direction behind her. "It's in an awkward spot . . ."

"Come on," he said, rising to his feet and stretching out a hand. "I imagine I can doctor you—I saw it all in Vietnam."

Blushing, she took his hand and let him pull her to her feet. They went inside.

He was wrong, however. He hadn't seen anything like that in Vietnam. If he had, he never would have come home.

EIGHT

Charlotte came out of the bathroom, wearing the giant towel she'd found in the linen closet. She was still numb from the shock of the fire, but like a hand on her body, Sam's warming scrutiny fell heavily upon her naked shoulders, forcing her attention into the present. She clutched the knotted towel at her breasts and stared at the lounging man across the room. He sat on the edge of his bed with his legs casually crossed, bandages and antiseptic spread out on the coverlet beside him.

While she'd showered, so had he. Now, the scent of his light aftershave drifted across the bed, replacing the smell of smoke she thought she couldn't forget and increasing her pulse. Somewhere in the front of the house, the old Lena Horne song she'd heard the day she'd fainted played on. Had he set the scene for seduction? Despite the fright she'd just had, or maybe because of it, she knew the time had come to face her attraction.

"I feel very uncomfortable with this," she said, believing that was how she *should* feel. "Don't you think we should get Myrtle or one of the other ladies to help me?"

Sam looked pointedly at the black-banded watch on his thick wrist. "It's almost two in the morning, Charlotte. I don't think they'd appreciate being awakened to play doctor."

She grimaced and tried to pull the towel up, desperate to cover more of her chest. All she did was reveal more of her legs. He was right, but that still didn't ease her disquiet.

Sam's blue eyes didn't miss her action. When his gaze rose to her face again, he grinned and patted the bed. "Come on, lie down. After all, it's not like I've never seen you without all your clothes on."

She compressed her lips. "Must you continually remind me of that?"

"Oh, relax, for Pete's sake." Again, he patted the bed beside him. "Come over here. I'll fix you up in no time."

That's exactly what I'm worried about, she thought to herself, moving reluctantly toward the enormous bed.

He stood up as she approached, and Charlotte was struck again by his size. When they weren't together, she remembered him as a tall and imposing man. When they stood side by side, she realized they were very close to the same height, but something about him made him seem larger. Maybe it was the skimpiness of the clothes he always wore.

He'd changed into black nylon running shorts. As he waited for her, arms crossed, Charlotte couldn't help but notice how incredibly masculine he looked. A slit, almost to his hip, in the side of the already brief shorts exposed long, tanned legs. As always, his chest was bare.

The brevity of his clothing seemed to emphasize her own lack of covering even more, and she pulled once again at the knot in the towel as she eased down to the edge of the bed. A sharp stinging pain took her attention from him. "Ouch!" was followed by a colorful oath.

"Roll over," Sam instructed, "and keep your legs out straight. It won't hurt so much."

Charlotte did as he instructed, pulling her bottom lip in between her teeth, muttering to herself all the time.

"Where did you learn to cuss?" Sam asked, easing the towel up from her seat as she stretched out. "It doesn't exactly seem to go with your personality."

"My dad's only legacy, I guess," she said tightly. Changing the subject before he could ask more, she continued. "How's it look?"

His eyes registered the minor injury then went on to take in the ivory skin glowing beneath the diaphanous peach silk of her underwear. Damn fine, Sam thought to himself. In fact, better than anything I've seen in a helluva long time. On her left cheek, she had a tiny, heart-shaped freckle, and Sam had the strangest urge to—

"Is it bad?" she pressed.

With his pulse throbbing at his temples, he forced his eyes to return to the dark bruise forming at the very top of her thigh, under the curve of her left buttock. The tender skin around it was red and scraped as if she'd been flung off a merry-go-round. His voice came out rougher than he intended. "Hell, no. It's just a little scratch, that's all. I'll clean it, then bandage it. You'll be fine."

He grabbed the bottle of antiseptic and flipped open the top. Without further warning, he squirted the cold liquid all over her upper leg.

"Holy sh—" Her oath was cut off as she clenched her teeth and jerked her head around to stare at him with accusing gray eyes. "That burns. Why didn't you warn me?"

She'd raised up slightly to deliver her complaint, her fingers clutching the wrinkled bedspread, her hair fanning over her shoulders like a velvet shawl. From his vantage point, Sam had a view of one rounded breast, barely hidden but still managing to tempt him like an apple from Eve's garden. If he got her really mad, she might just jump up completely. He held out the white bottle. "Do you want to do this yourself?"

She tightened her lips and stared at him angrily for two seconds. Finally, she shook her head. "Just hurry up," she said in a contentious voice and turned around. "I don't like lying here on your bed with my underwear on."

"Which part don't you like? Lying here or lying here *in your underwear*? I'm sure I could arrange for something different," he said calmly, picking up the large, square Band-Aid beside him. "I could take off—"

"I'd like you to finish what you're doing and let me go to bed," she interrupted. "I've had a rough night, damnit, and I'm tired. Racing down four flights of stairs with a hundred panicked people, breathing in smoke, falling down on my butt . . ." She took a deep breath then continued her harangue. "Having you play doctor while I can't do anything about it, isn't exactly ending the evening on a pleasant note, either. So just hurry up and finish the job, damnit to hell."

For just a moment, Sam felt like saluting. He hadn't had anyone deliver a set of instructions quite so succinctly since he'd retired. Instead, he slapped the Band-Aid across the top of her thigh and pressed the edges into her skin, trying like hell to avoid feeling the smooth satin beneath his rough fingers.

"All right," he said finally, his voice as cold as he could make it. "The job is finished. I hope it's to your satisfaction."

Like a felon just freed from jail, Charlotte jumped up from the bed, clutching the towel in front of her chest. "Thank you very much," she snapped. "You're a real Dr. Kildare." She stared at him a second longer, then collapsed on the bed, instantly bursting into tears.

Horrified, Sam looked at the shaking, bawling woman in front of him. Had he been too rough? Had he said something wrong?

Suddenly, the realization hit him. Death *had* been too close to her tonight. Nothing was more frightening than a fire, and the shakes were setting in now that it was over.

Charlotte felt like an idiot, but her tears refused to stop. She'd made it through the fire, gotten herself to Sam's, suffered through his comments, and now—now—she was crying like a ten-year-old kid. Heedless of what she was doing, she pulled up the towel she'd been clutching and covered her face in its pristine whiteness. Vaguely she heard Sam speak above her sobs. His arm went around her shoulder.

Dropping the towel to her breasts, she turned and buried her face against the wall of his chest. His hand cradled the back of her head as he murmured softly. She cried until she couldn't get out another tear. Sniffing, she finally raised her head and stared at him.

"I . . . I'm sorry," she said. "I don't know what happened. I usually don't cry like that, but . . ."

His blue eyes stared down at her in the faint light of the lamp beside the bed. "It's okay." His voice was a gruff absolution. "I've seen tough guys cry over less, believe me."

She dabbed at her eyes with the towel. "It's more than just the fire. It's coming down here, trying to fix my mistakes, sorting out my confusion—"

"Your confusion?"

"Yes, over everything. My whole damn life is a mess, what with Jonathan, and now you, and—"

Horrified, she broke off, looked up quickly then dropped her eyes again. The heavy arm around her shoulder, that only moments before had been reassuring, now suddenly seemed very uncomfortable as he tightened his grip.

"I think breaking up with Jonathan was probably the smartest thing you've done in a long time."

"I . . . I thought so at the time, too," she said. "But, damnit, I'm scared now." She breathed deeply, her heart doing the fifty-yard dash inside her chest. "When he touched me, wh . . . when you touch me . . ."

"It didn't feel the same?"

His hands were like warm gold against her bare skin; dark, smooth, polished. She wanted to shiver, but his eyes, his hot-blue eyes, held hers and refused to let her move an inch.

"Yes," she whispered, closing her eyes, unable to stop him, yet helpless to move. "Like that . . ."

With strong fingers, he gently massaged the muscles of her shoulders, working them as if he were playing the piano, feeling for just the right strength, for just the right place. Charlotte felt her resistance disappear.

As if he'd sensed her acquiescence, Sam's fingers tightened against her shoulders and pulled her to him. "Then let me show you more, Charlotte," he breathed. She wanted to protest, but he bent his head to hers and covered her mouth with his lips.

The shock of his kiss radiated down her body, sending wave after wave of delicious pressure coursing over her. Surprise gave over to instant pleasure, and without even being aware of having a choice in the matter, Charlotte found herself responding.

Dropping her towel, Charlotte's hands snaked up to his neck. As though she'd walked into the surf pounding the shore outside the bedroom door, she was swamped with an enveloping passion. Curling her fingers through the softness of his hair to the corded muscles beneath, Charlotte pressed the length of her body against Sam's. He groaned into her open mouth and cradled her throat with his right hand, his thumb on her chin. He threaded the fingers of his left hand into her heavy, dark hair. With a rumble of desire, he insinuated his tongue into her mouth.

Her breath coming hot and fast, Charlotte pressed her bare breasts against his chest, the tips rubbing almost painfully against his coarse hair. His hands moved from her face to her shoulders, traced down her sides, then rose once more to cup the heaviness between them. With his thumb, he brushed her nipples into hard spots of pleasure. Like circles from a skipping stone, desire rippled over her. His touch was rough and exciting, different from anything she'd ever experienced before.

No kiss had prepared her for the attack now taking place against her senses. Sam's weapons were formidable; his tactics flawless.

Joining the game, Charlotte parried the thrust of Sam's tongue with one of her own. Darting, teasing, probing touches that seemed to arouse him as much as they excited her. Convulsively, her hands tightened against his neck, then trailed down his back.

Finally, he tore his mouth from hers, his lips marking a heated path down the line of her jaw. Deep in the back of her throat, a moan built from a passion that had smoldered for far too long. When his teeth nipped gently at the swell of her breasts, Charlotte found herself arching backwards. Together, they tumbled back across the bed, Sam scrambling to remove his shorts.

Stretched out beside her, Sam raised his face to stare at her. His pupils were wide with desire, centers of black with magnetic blue rims. They almost seemed to pulse with an energy, a passion—a desire she didn't know how to contain. Suddenly she was scared, but she didn't want to stop. Tightening her grip on his arms, she drew him closer.

Deliberately, slowly, his eyes never leaving hers, Sam

resisted, pulling away from her but keeping his own hands hard against her upper arms.

She swallowed hard. "W . . . what's wrong?"

His fingers contracted against her arms. "Do you want me?" he said roughly.

Her breath stopped. "Yes," she whispered in wonderment. Her gaze fell to his chest. Tiny swirls of bronzed hair begged for her fingers, but she kept still, her palms growing moist around his neck. "I do. I want you like no other man I've ever wanted."

"Good," he said roughly. "Because I'm going to be the last man you'll *ever* want."

He kissed her again, plunging his tongue into her mouth, whispering against her lips, telling her exactly what he was going to do and how she was going to like it. She pulled in her breath, shocked but mesmerized; no man had ever talked to her like that, and she found it unbearably exciting. As her astonishment slacked and her ardor grew, Charlotte responded the only way she knew how, by clutching his shoulders and thrusting her hips against his, moaning with growing desire.

With a primal cry, Sam tumbled her back against the mattress, holding both of her wrists in one of his hands. Pulling off her silk underwear, he stretched her out, then began a slow, passionate torture.

He didn't make love like she expected. His laid back attitude, his easygoing posture, his devil-may-care stance all disappeared—evaporated in the heat of his intensity. Talking to her all the while, he covered her body with kisses, his mouth and hands eliciting sensations totally new to Charlotte.

With one hand at her side, his lips stopped at the peaks of her breasts, teasing, pulling, sucking her into the warm wetness of his mouth while his palm went lower to cup her gently in the center of his hand. His fingers stayed still, but the fire building inside of her flamed even higher, and she squirmed against him, seeking more, wanting more.

He ignored her unspoken request, rotating his hand against her but still holding back as his lips continued to seek her breast. With hands growing desperate, Charlotte clutched at his bare back and moaned once more.

Tearing his mouth away, Sam seared her with the blue flame of his eyes. "Do you like that?" he said, "or would you rather I—"

"Please, Sam," she breathed, looking at him through half-closed lids.

"Please what?" he teased unmercifully.

She pushed herself against his fingers, then gasped as he answered her plea, feathering his touch over her so lightly, so gently that she could only cry for more. Pressing his lips once again to her breast, he probed deeper with his hand, stroking her with a rhythm older than both of them. Her fingernails dug into the muscles of his shoulder as she tensed—consumed with the fire of his touch—then shuddered into stillness.

Slowly, he drew his hand away, lifted his mouth from her body and rose up on his elbows. Like the waves crashing on the shore outside, the tension between them ebbed, then increased. He gently parted her legs with one of his knees. Staring at her with eyes that seemed to glow in the darkened bedroom, he moved his weight between her legs.

She tensed, waiting for him to lower his body to hers, but instead he went to his knees between her legs. Their eyes locked. Sam lifted her right leg and then her left to his shoulders.

Charlotte gasped and tried to pull back, but he wouldn't let her. "Relax, baby," he whispered, lowering his face to the juncture of her thighs, "and keep your ankles high."

With an inarticulate moan, she let her head fall back against the pillows and closed her eyes, too far gone now to care. Instantly, his tongue parted her and the teasing, light kisses began all over again.

Charlotte's hands grabbed Sam's thick blond hair as her body rocked with his loving. Nothing in her life had ever prepared her for the response she felt to this man. When she knew she could stand no more, he rose.

She opened her eyes and stared at him as her legs slid down over his back and locked above his buttocks. With a savage cry, he plunged inside of her and the storm began all over again.

For endless moments, Charlotte rose to meet him, all the desires she'd held back now releasing in a world filled only with passion. He buried his face against her neck, breathing her name over and over as they rocked in unison. Finally, they both trembled into stillness, their harsh breathing filling the bedroom with the dying sounds of passion. Several moments later, Sam raised up and looked at her in the darkness. Underneath her hand, resting on his chest, Charlotte could feel the slowing beat of his heart.

"Did that feel," he paused and grinned, "like it should?"

She answered him with a smile and a kiss, then shook her head. "No," she answered, "it felt better than it should."

The pillow beneath her face smelled too much like Sam, the imprint of his fingers still lingered on her wrists, and the sheets were far too tangled as the morning sun broke the horizon, bringing Charlotte to total awareness. Her eyes flew open to see Punch, sitting in the middle of the twisted sheets and barking twice, as if to ask what she was doing there.

"I'm not too sure myself," she answered, then raised up on one elbow and surveyed the wide bed, pushing her hair back from her face with a sleep-slowed hand. The only sign of Sam was a huge T-shirt at the foot of the mattress, but she heard kitchen sounds from the front of the condo.

Ignoring the gentle soreness in her body and the noise of pots and pans, she eased slowly from the bed and grabbed the shirt, slipping it over her head as she walked to the covered windows then pulled back the heavily lined drapes. Sunlight poured into the room, and she took a deep breath, opening the sliding glass door. There was no time she liked better than early morning.

Wandering to the built-in bench that surrounded the small deck, Charlotte sank to the cushioned frame and pulled her feet up beside her. Tucking her legs in under the T-shirt, she wrapped her arms around them and rested her chin on her kneecaps.

The beach was silent, the sand washed clean of footsteps by the gentle rain that had fallen after they'd finally gone to sleep. A raging storm would have been more appropriate, she thought silently. A hurricane, in fact, something that could rival the feelings Sam had fired inside of her.

Sam Gibson was not her kind of man. They were oil and water, day and night, hard and soft.

So why in hell had she made love with him—if you could call what they'd done making love. It had seemed more like a battle. But one, she had to admit, she'd be willing to fight again—and again. She shook her head in amazement. She'd never liked men who didn't shave, men who didn't work, men who were so, well, so masculine. Why now? Why Sam Gibson?

She stared out at the emerald water as if the answers to her questions could be heard in the rhythmic sounds of the waves. The reverberating harmony of water against shore told her nothing, however.

Pink streaks of sunlight were reaching out across the sky now, and in another twenty minutes the day would begin in earnest. The beach would be covered with tourists, the tourists would be covered with sunblock, and she would be covered in work. Today, she'd have to do more than see to the repair of the condos. She'd have to repair her state of mind and find a place to live for a few more weeks. She'd have to call the bank, and tell Jonathan what had happened—about the fire, that is, she amended quickly in her mind. The thought of hearing his cold voice after the night of passion she'd just experienced wasn't something she was looking forward to.

Behind her, the sliding glass door whispered open, and Sam emerged. Wearing a bright blue bathing suit and nothing more, he silently set down two steaming mugs of coffee, took her chin in his hand and tilted her face up. Cupping her cheek with his hand, he bent, his kiss swift but deep, then straightened back up, taking her breath with him as he went. A whiff of aftershave lingered, and she couldn't help but smile as she took in his smooth jawline.

He sat down opposite her and grinned. "There's a lot of things I know about you, Charlotte Huntington, but how you like your coffee isn't one of them." He nodded toward the steaming brew. "I guessed black."

"Perfect," she answered, shyly avoiding his gaze. In the bright sunlight, it was hard for her to accept the things they'd shared in the darkness of the night before, especially with the thought of Jonathan fresh on her mind. Silently, she sipped the coffee.

He broke her silence. "So, tell me some more so I won't have to guess the rest."

Her gray eyes stared at him over the rim of her mug. Sam stared back, telling himself the funny rumble in his stomach was a lack of breakfast. She shrugged. "What do you want to know?"

"Everything—but you can start with your childhood."

"That's history. You don't want to hear it."

He reached out and took her chin in his hand, his fingers fanning against her cheek. "Charlotte, we shared something last night, something unique. Now, I don't know about you, but I plan on sharing it again, and I don't share something like that with strangers."

Her eyes dropped, but not before he saw the glint of moisture in them. "I . . . I didn't have a happy childhood, and I don't feel comfortable explaining it all."

He crossed his arms. "So, feel uncomfortable."

She threw him a rueful grin. "You're awfully persistent."

He nodded. "Yes. That's one of the things the military teaches you."

"Oh, really?" She lifted her eyebrows. "Is that what got you a presidential commendation?"

His blue eyes cut to her face. "How'd you find that out?"

"The day I used your telephone, I accidentally knocked over the box under the bed. Your medals came out, and . . ."

"And you snooped?"

"I'm afraid so."

He reached out and caught a dark brown curl between his fingers, then brought it to his nose. The silky hair held her fragrance. "That's okay. I guess there aren't too many secrets between us now. Are there?" He smiled slowly, then pulled gently on the curl. "You're not going to distract me that easily, though. Tell me—everytime I mention your dad you freeze. What did he do that was so awful?"

"Besides kill himself?" She blinked rapidly and looked as though she wished she'd stayed quiet, then turned her head to stare out at the glassy sea, pulling her hair from his hand. She continued to avoid his eyes. "There's nothing else to tell."

"Or nothing else you *want* to tell?"

"His death was very painful for me, Sam."

"You don't blame yourself, do you?"

"No, not really, but I've always felt like there was something missing, something I should have done that I didn't." She turned to face him, her wide grey eyes a mirror of the morning sky. "Does that make any sense?"

"Perfect sense to me." He sipped his coffee. "I felt a little like that when my parents were killed; actually, I think everyone has that sense of unfinished business when someone they love dies quickly."

She nodded, ducking her head to sip from her coffee. When she raised her eyes again, they were moist with unshed tears. "When I was a kid, I always felt like he loved my brother more than me. They went hunting together every fall, played ball in the spring, went fishing in the summer. I did everything I could to prove to him how great I was, too—that I deserved some attention, also—but he never noticed, and when he died, I knew I'd never get the chance again."

Sam leaned back against the cushions lining the deck and sipped his coffee. "How did it happen?" he asked quietly.

She wrapped her fingers around the steaming mug and stared out over the water. "After the divorce, he really hit the booze; after the discharge, he couldn't control it at all. One night, he drove to the NCO club, stumbled out into the parking lot, and pulled a pistol out from under the seat of his car. They heard the shot from inside the club, went out, and found him sprawled across the hood."

"I'm sorry."

She shook her head, her eyes filling with tears. Sam

had the impression this was the first time she'd been able to cry for the man she'd loved so much.

His heart cracked open at the sight of her long-held pain. "What about your mom?" he asked softly.

"She eventually remarried, but she passed away about five years ago. Heart attack."

"So, all you've got is your brother."

"Yes. We speak at Christmas, that's about it." Her lips pursed, and she looked almost apologetic. "I guess I've always resented him, to be truthful. I know that doesn't sound too good, but it was hard not to when I was a kid, and I've held on to those feelings a little longer than necessary."

He reached out and ran a finger down her jaw line. "Families are important. If you talked to him, I'd be willing to bet that he saw your childhood a helluva lot different than you did."

She leaned into his touch, then looked up at him. "What about yours? Tell me about the Sam Gibson who was a kid. I bet you were meaner than hell."

"Nope. My grandparents wouldn't let me." He shook his head. "They were very strict, but I didn't appreciate that until after I joined the service, and they had died." Dropping his hand, he looked into his coffee cup. "I'm all alone. No uncles, no aunts, no nieces, no nephews. Nothing."

"I . . . I didn't realize . . ."

He smiled into her eyes. "That's why I like all the old people around here. They've adopted me, and I've adopted them. It works out, actually." He frowned, a look of mock concern. "Thank God we're not actually related. If insanity was hereditary, I'd be in trouble."

"They do seem pretty, uh, interesting," she agreed.

"They have a community poker game going this afternoon. The stakes are usually pretty high but if you want in, they might cut you some slack. If you'd rather, we can play golf, sit on the beach, take a ride down to the park—what would you like?"

"Sam," she said gently, shaking her head. "I have work to do. Remember?"

For one second, their eyes clashed before he carefully set down his mug. "I thought you might—"

"No," she broke in awkwardly. "I have the painter coming, and the wallpaper woman promised she'd be here today, too." She looked down at her bare finger, the spasm of guilt she obviously felt clear on her face. "I have a deadline, you know, and Jonathan *is* still my boss. . . ."

Leaning across the cushion toward her, Sam picked up her hand. "Yes," he said smoothly. "Your boss, but nothing more. Right?"

"Yes," she said with a firm expression. "Nothing more."

Dropping her fingers, he reached out and tucked a strand of her hair behind her ear, his thumb outlining the edge of her ear as he shook his head. "Well, if you insist on working, then we'll share lunch. How's that?"

She grinned. "Nothing more?"

He answered her tease with one of his own. "I'd be happy to arrange for *more*, if that's what you'd like."

"I'm not sure I could handle it." Her words were light, but he had no trouble deciphering the seriousness behind them.

He bent his head to her lips. "Then, I'll make you sure."

For several endless moments, he kissed her. When he raised his head, her eyes were glazed with desire, but almost instantly, she blinked the violent hunger away. "I don't want to get swept away on the moment, Sam."

"Why not? Sometimes you need to get swept away."

She gently pushed him back, her small hands warm

against his bare chest. When their eyes met once more, Sam read her resolution in their clear, gray depths, even before she shook her head. "I'm not into . . ."

"Flings?" he supplied.

Her cheeks darkened. "If that's the word you want to use." She lifted her shoulders, a pained expression on her face. "I need more than that, want more than that. I have to have stability, Sam, that's very important to me. A house in the suburbs, TV after dinner, lights out at ten. It sounds corny, but that's what I didn't have as a child, and it's what I have to have as an adult."

Sam captured her hands between his. "You want that more than what I gave you last night?"

Her eyes fell to their tangled fingers as if she were remembering the hours of pleasure they'd shared, but she shook her head, still refusing to meet his gaze. "Not more—but as much."

"Are you sure? You had stability with Jonathan and you gave it up."

"Yes," she whispered, "I know. He wasn't the right man, but what he represented is what I still want."

His voice was rough with honesty. "I think that's what you *think* you want. I'm not sure that's reality."

"Maybe not," she acknowledged, "but Jonathan was the kind of man my father never was, and that's what I've always looked for in a husband."

Sam lifted her chin with two fingers and looked into her soul. "Maybe you've been looking for the wrong things, baby."

Myrtle leaned over the short fence in front of her unit and eyed Sam with undisguised surprise, her cigarette dangling from one side of her mouth. "What happened? The lady banker threaten to sue you if you didn't get your ass in gear?"

He leaned back on his heels and grinned above the newly repaired sidewalk. "No. I was afraid you'd fall down and break yours." He stared back down at the board and shook his head. "Look at that! It took me a whole hour just to put in one little ole board."

She took a long drag from the cigarette, then pulled it out of her mouth and stared at the inch-long ash before tapping it on the fence. "Yep—that's what happens when you ain't got your mind on your work."

Sam eyed her suspiciously. "What makes you think my mind isn't where it should be?"

She crammed the cigarette back between her lips and spoke out the side of her mouth. "I happened to be up last night, couldn't sleep—old people have that problem, you know—and I saw Ms. Huntington arrive on your doorstep in her fancy nightie." She narrowed her watery eyes and looked at Sam through a haze of smoke as if she knew some secret he didn't.

"So?"

"Well, it didn't hide much, honey. I figure any man who has a woman like that in his apartment all night wouldn't have his mind on his work the next day. No matter which way it turned out." Her cackled laugh died with a short coughing spell.

Sam grinned, then explained about the fire with as few words as possible. Myrtle's blue eyes widened into ovals of alarm. "Was anyone hurt?"

"No, thank God. Charlotte was really shook up, though. I can understand why, too. Nothing is more frightening than a fire."

Myrtle puffed and looked at him. "She gonna stay with you now?"

"I wish," he said without thinking. As soon as the words were out, however, he realized how much he would like just that kind of arrangement. Charlotte, however, would never see things that way; she was far too prim and proper—or at least, that was the image she liked to project. He knew better now. "She's on the phone right now, trying to find another hotel to—"

Just as he spoke, the door to his unit opened, and Charlotte walked out.

A collage of images registered in his mind, all at one time; a dark sundress that revealed bare, ivory shoulders and shadowy, deep cleavage; silky hair in a loose knot on top of her head; a fresh face devoid of makeup and looking five years younger for its absence; and finally, long, white legs free of hose and feet unconfined by shoes.

Smelling sweetly of gardenias, Charlotte glided to a halt in front of him and said hello to Myrtle. When Sam was finally able to pull his eyes to her face, he realized she wore a look of distress. Her grey eyes were tight with worry, and double lines, faint but noticeable, ran from the corners of her mouth.

Myrtle must have observed the same signs. "Sorry about your trouble last night," she offered. "Must have scared you half to death."

Charlotte nodded. "It did. I'm glad no one was hurt, though." She grimaced slightly, "Well, almost no one."

Myrtle raised her penciled eyebrows and stared at Charlotte through a haze of smoke. With a guilty start, Sam broke in, his voice gruff. He hadn't even inquired about her injury. "How is it this morning?"

Myrtle's eyes bounced to Sam's face then back to Charlotte's. "Not bad," she said, "still kinda sore. I can't sit down real good."

Myrtle's eyebrows went up another notch.

"Do you need another bandage?"

"No, I think this one's big enough. It kinda itches, though."

Like a spectator watching a tennis match, Myrtle's face turned back to Sam's as she waited for his answer.

He grinned, unable to hold back. "I'd be happy to scratch it for you."

Myrtle, faded eyes round with curiosity, whipped her head back toward Charlotte's direction.

"I don't believe that will be necessary."

Every time they'd spoken, Myrtle had taken another drag on her cigarette. Now smoke hung between the three of them in the humid Florida sun. Myrtle squinted at Sam, waiting for his answer. Charlotte put a nervous hand to the top of her dress and pulled.

Finally, Sam shrugged his shoulders and pretended to direct his attention to the new sidewalk.

"Where you goin' live, sweetheart?" Myrtle asked.

"I don't know," Charlotte replied. "I've called every hotel in town, and nothing's available. The Shriners have filled up almost everything, and a convention of romance writers took the rest." Her voice dropped another notch. "I don't know what I'm going to do, frankly. I need to be as close as possible to the project to oversee the subs."

"Well, hell's bells, honey—why don't you stay here?"

Charlotte stiffened noticeably. "What?"

Myrtle nodded her head enthusiastically, her cigarette losing its ash in the process. "Why not?" She pointed to the project over her shoulder. "They may not be in perfect condition, but they're empty. You'd be right here to supervise your workers, and you could keep a real close eye on them."

Sam held his breath.

Charlotte rested one coral-tipped finger against her chin. "You know, Myrtle, that's not a bad suggestion. I'd save the bank some money, too." She smiled brightly. "I don't know why I didn't think of that earlier. Thanks for the help!"

When the door closed behind her, Sam turned to Myrtle, his eyes teasing. "Thanks a bunch. Now she'll be here all the time, making sure I work, getting in my hair night and day."

Myrtle's cheeks sunk in as she pulled on her cigarette. Tilting her head up to the sun, she blew out the smoke. "Yeah—and that's just what you want, ain't it?"

NINE

In a matter of days, the project looked like an ant pile that had just gotten the boot, the subs running in and out of the condos like crazed insects. The exterior of Safe Harbor still needed some work, but the interiors of the bank's units were taking on a whole new look.

Standing in the den of the only three-bedroom unit, Charlotte breathed deeply. The smell of fresh paint was sharp in her nostrils, but it signified progress, and she didn't mind the fumes. Walking closer to one of the door frames, she saw something she did mind, however—sloppy work. She flipped open her notebook, jotted a quick notation, then peeled off a bright orange sticker, and slapped it on the offending wall. In the morning, she'd point out the mistake to the painter.

Most of the remodeling had been going well, however. A constant parade of workers dodged the old people who looked on in amazement, offered free advice, and pilfered anything the subs didn't take home at night. Everyone was happy, though; the tenants liked the excitement, the workers liked the attention, and Punch liked all the empty food cartons the workers left lying around.

Wandering back to the bedrooms, Charlotte had to admit she was happiest of all. She loved being out of the office, organizing the workers, arranging for materials to be delivered, accomplishing what she'd been sent to do. The work was vastly more satisfying than her job at the bank. There, it seemed she only shuffled paper. Here, she could see obvious results. The only problem was Sam.

Every time she looked up, he was there, either staring at her with those incredible eyes, riding in on his motorcycle, or heading for the beach in his swimsuit . . . doing everything but working.

In fact, since she'd moved in, she'd done less work, too. Sam constantly distracted her, either by his presence or by his memory. The nights were long in Florida, and he'd been filling hers with more than just dreams.

She stepped into the master bedroom and let her eyes roam over the newly hung wallpaper. Instead of concentrating on the seams, however, she found her thoughts centering on Sam and the goals she wanted to reach.

A family, a husband, real commitment, not to mention her career—those were things that were important to her. She hadn't asked, but she knew that Sam didn't think much of those aspirations. He'd accomplished his goals, and now he only wanted to play.

She had to admit, though, Sam had taught her how to have fun, and she felt more alive now than she ever had. Colors were brighter, the sun was warmer, kisses were deeper—all thanks to Sam Gibson.

A trapped fly, angrily buzzing against the glass, broke her reverie, and Charlotte turned to leave. Sam had her cornered as neatly as the glass did the fly, and she knew it.

The question was—what was she going to do about it?

*   *   *

She hadn't worn the black sundress again. Sam knew. He watched for it everyday. And everyday, he'd been disappointed.

Today she wore khaki shorts with knife-edged creases and a white cotton blouse as she stood outside his porch and talked earnestly with the painter. Her sleeves were rolled up and her hair was twisted neatly into a bun at the back of her neck. One small, dark curl kissed the damp skin above her collar. Her legs—those incredible, long legs—were beginning to turn a delicious shade of apricot from being in the Florida sun every day for several weeks.

Sam padded closer to the screen surrounding his porch and eavesdropped on the conversation taking place.

"I've placed stickers—orange stickers, you can't miss them—everywhere I found unacceptable work," she was saying, her voice school-teacher prim. "You may correct the problems now or later, it doesn't matter to me as long as it's done by our deadline."

The coffee Sam swallowed suddenly seemed to go down the wrong way. Charlotte had hired the best painter in Destin—Sam knew him—and he was extremely proud of his work, but he hadn't been nicknamed Tiger Garcia for no reason at all.

He towered over Charlotte, an imposing figure with his long black hair pulled back into a ponytail and dark sunglasses wrapping around his pock-marked face. When he wasn't in jail, he got most of the work in town. Sam held his breath as Tiger put his hands on his hips and glared at her.

"Unacceptable?" he growled. "What do you mean unacceptable?"

Charlotte glanced down at the notebook in her hands. "Around the door frames in Unit 3B, the trim work is sloppy. In number 2A, you completely skipped the area behind the cabinets in the bathroom, and in 4D—''

"What do you want, for God's sake? Perfection? I'm the best damn—''

She flushed and held up her hand. "I don't appreciate being sworn at, Mr. Garcia.''

Sam sputtered hot coffee over the screen. How in the world could she say something like that? She talked like a sailor when she got angry!

"And furthermore, I do not accept sloppy work. I was told you were an excellent painter, but frankly, I find your work less than satisfactory. The bank will not pay you until I am pleased. You might want to keep that in mind.''

Garcia moved a step closer, and Sam's body tensed. Charlotte stood her ground as the painter bent his face into hers. "You might want to keep this in mind, little lady. I can walk off this job anytime I like and leave you with a big problem. You'll be begging me to come back.'' His paint-flecked hand came up to grab her jaw. "In fact, you might just be begging me to do something besides paint your houses, and believe me, I'd enjoy that a helluva lot more.''

Charlotte jerked her head to one side and Sam's anger exploded. Instantly, he slammed his coffee cup down and threw open the back door, rage fueling his feet as he covered the space between them and his porch in two swift steps.

At Sam's appearance, Garcia froze in surprise, his fingers still digging into the soft skin of Charlotte's face. Before the painter could drop his hand, Sam grabbed his arm, twisted it behind his back, and shoved him to the ground, straddling the man like a bull dogger at a rodeo. For two seconds, the painter stayed still with surprise, then he began to struggle in earnest.

"What in the hell do you think you're doing, you crazy son-of-a—"

The curse ended in another howl as Sam jerked the arm higher. "Can it, Garcia. Didn't you hear the lady? She doesn't like cussing."

With wide, stormy eyes, Charlotte stared down at the two men in the grass, rubbing her fingers over the redness of her cheeks. "Sam—"

"You hush, too," he snapped then focused his attention back on the man beneath him. Sam didn't want to lose his concentration now; rumors said Garcia kept a knife handy. Sam bent closer to the painter, his voice an angry hiss. "If I ever see you around here again, you'll live to regret it. Do you understand me?"

A stream of Spanish invectives answered him. Sam pulled Garcia's arm again, and a painful yowl came back. He leaned down even closer so Charlotte couldn't hear. "And if you ever, *ever*, even think about this woman, much less *touch* her, you'll die and be glad. Do you understand me, *bastardo*?"

Sam stared down at Garcia's face. The one side that wasn't pressed into the sandy yard revealed a dark eye that grew wide at the Spanish insult. His whiskered jaw worked back and forth then finally he nodded. Sam released him, jumped back, then stared at the painter with every ounce of hate in his body. Gazing at him with dazed eyes, Garcia stumbled upright then cradled his right arm in his left hand. With a final shake of his head, the painter turned and lurched toward the parking lot, mumbling under his breath.

Sam turned to Charlotte. "Are you okay?"

Her eyes gleamed with excitement. "No one's ever stood up for me like that."

Like electricity, her exhilaration arced between them, and Sam responded, his hands on her arms, his lips against hers. He deliberately made the kiss a rough one, sensing in her the need.

She answered instantly, and losing the last bit of control he had, Sam slid his hand along her thigh, up under her shorts until she gasped and pushed him away. "Sam," she said, laboring to catch her breath, turning her head toward the condos. "Not here."

He flashed a glance toward the units. "You're right," he said. "Not here." He headed toward his condo with need driving every step, pulling her behind him.

At high speed, they entered his back porch, Sam pulling her inside, his momentum carrying her to the other side of the room as he stopped to close the door. From across the den, he turned and burned her with his eyes, then something inside of her broke. She was another woman— a primal, sensual woman who gave in to her emotions and passions—a woman who knew she was worth fighting for.

She beckoned. He came. Her own hands went around his neck, her fingers plowed into his thick, silky hair, pulling his mouth to hers. "I want you, Sam," she said, rising up to meet him.

His blue eyes seemed suddenly to ignite and he dipped his head, wrapped his arms around her, and brought his lips to hers. "Like this?" he murmured, his hand under her blouse. "Or like this?" Charlotte's heart stood still as their mouths met in an explosion of desire.

Instantly, Sam's tongue parted Charlotte's lips, a quick darting that left her wanting more. With a low moan, Charlotte pressed her hips against his body—a body that told her he, too, wanted more. He deepened the kiss, rubbing his hands up and down her bare arms, plunging his tongue with rhythmic urgency into the center of her mouth.

The mocking movement pushed her into an even deeper

level of desire, and Charlotte squirmed against his chest, wishing, and pressing, for more. With an aching groan, Sam tore his mouth from hers then slid his hands under her arms, his mouth tracing a line of fire from her lips to the neck of her blouse as he lifted her up, cupping her derriere with his hands.

With a tiny gasp of surprise, Charlotte clasped her arms around his neck and hung on, wrapping her legs around his waist and pulling him even closer, pressing herself hotly against his stomach. His waist was narrow, his hips slim, but the feverish hands holding her up were steady and strong.

With a growl of desire and desperation, Sam returned his hands to her hips and suddenly tightened his grip, whispering one hoarse request.

She moaned her agreement.

He was holding her even closer now, the heat of his desire matching her own, as he moved out of the porch and into the den. In two quick strides, he had her down on the couch, obviously not trusting himself to make it as far as the bedroom. Stripping his shirt from his back and his shorts from his hips, he lowered himself, pulsing with desire, to the edge of the cushions.

He buried his face in her neck, one hand at the buttons on her blouse. Instantly, he had them undone, and the front clasp of her bra quickly followed.

With lightning speed, his lips danced over her now-bare breasts, first one and then the other. Charlotte arched her back to accept the wet caresses of tongue and hand, her entire body straining until the pleasure was so great she thought she would pass out. Finally, he eased the torture, lifting his head momentarily to nuzzle between the aching fullness.

Her hands tightened in his hair as her tongue found one ear. She lathed the edge slowly, delicately until he shuddered with pent-up need. "Oh, God," he breathed, "Don't stop. Don't stop."

She had no intention of stopping—now or later as her hands glided down his back then tightened and pulled him even closer.

With shaking hands, he grabbed the waistband of her shorts and tugged. After a soft whimper of need, she lifted her hips, clutching his arms with fingers that were made of steel. A second later, sheer peach panties followed.

Staring at her, Sam was astonished again by the beauty of her body. No wonder she wanted perfection in everything else—she had it already with herself.

He bent his face into the sweet valley between her breasts, breathing in her spicy perfume as she tangled her hands in his hair. Reveling in the softness of her ivory skin, he placed his palms on either side of her fullness, pressing his face against the fragrant orbs. She groaned as he raised his mouth to take in first one nipple and then the other, teasing with his lips, pulling with his teeth, making promises he couldn't wait to keep.

He slid his hand down the silky smoothness of her stomach, to the softness of her legs, then back up again, the texture of her skin exceeding even his fantasies. As his mouth trailed behind his hand, Charlotte murmured her growing need. When his lips found their target, she cried out in a different way.

Rising once more, Sam stared at her flushed and glowing face. Their eyes locked. Her voice husky with passion, she asked him the same question he'd mocked her with before. "Do you want me, Sam?"

He nodded and she spoke again. "Then tell me," she whispered. "Tell me you want me."

He lowered his body to hers, settled between her thighs, and entered her, breathing into her ear. "I'm not going to tell you, baby. I'm going to show you." With a gentle thrust, he silenced her words of hoarse need, his voice cracking with pleasure as he followed through with his promise. Instantly, her cries mingled with his.

TEN

"Why don't you stay at my place tonight? I want to sleep with you and to wake up next to you. To see your hair spread out across my pillow. . . ."

Sam's low, liquid voice sent shivers up Charlotte's back as he drew circles against her bare skin with one fingertip.

"Not tonight," she answered, barely dodging the coil of desire waiting to tie her up again. "I . . . I have some thinking to do."

"Go ahead and think." He nibbled along her neck, then raised his face to look at her. "I don't need your brain—just your body."

Automatically, Charlotte pulled her breath in, releasing it slowly as she saw his mocking grin "You're incorrigible, you know that?"

He smiled, "Yeah, and you love every minute of it, don't you?"

In the background, she heard the soothing sounds of the seashore, water against sand, birds against the air. A gentle breeze rattled a nearby set of wind chimes, the lonely tinkling sounding only half as forlorn as usual with Sam's arms around her.

"Yeah," she finally answered, echoing his casual tone. "And that's exactly what I have to think about."

He looked down at her. "Can't you just let it be, Charlotte? Can't you just accept what we have—enjoy it—feel it—relish it, right here and now?"

"When my job here is finished, I have to return to Denver." She put a heavy hand against his chest, his pulse throbbing beneath her fingers. "It bothers me to think our relationship is a temporary one."

"It doesn't have to be."

Charlotte licked suddenly dry lips. "I have a life in Denver."

"You've had more of one here." His eyes burned into hers. "Are you ready to give that up?"

"I have to think about it," she said. "I can't just relinquish everything I've worked so hard for—you know how much my career means to me." She dropped her eyes. "I have to think about all the options."

"Why do you have to analyze it?" He stared down at her in the hazy afternoon light. "Why can't you simply take the situation for what it is, and not worry about the future?"

In the circle of his arms, she stiffened. "Because that's the way I am, Sam. I don't know why, but I have to know which way I'm headed—to understand my feelings."

A pensive frown drew his brows together. "Understand or control?"

"Both? I'm not sure. Is that so wrong?"

He bent his head down and covered her lips in a short, blazing kiss, then lifted his face to pierce her eyes with his. "You tell me—after you've thought about it."

The work continued on the condos, but Charlotte could only think of Sam. He filled her days with laughter and her nights with passion. The thought of giving all that up, of returning to Denver, hovered constantly in the back of her mind. Even though she knew Sam would never provide her with everything she was looking for, still she wondered. A permanent relationship was what she needed, but what about him? What did he want?

She couldn't bring herself to ask because she was afraid of the answer. Instead, she focused on what he did best—living.

"I . . . I've never been on a motorcycle before." Charlotte stared at the huge, black monster in front of her, then flicked her eyes back to Sam. He'd come to take her to lunch, but she was having second, and third, thoughts. "Are you sure you can handle it with both of us on it?"

Sam stretched his long legs out, his boots kicking up small puffs of dust. "I gave you a pretty good ride the other night, and you didn't fall off." He grinned and held out his hand. "Trust me."

Margaret and Sissy were outside pruning their roses—the way they were snickering, they'd probably heard everything. She shot a glance toward the women, then waved in what she hoped was a casual way as she saw them staring. They waved back. She turned back to Sam, her face a deep red, her hand at her throat. "Please, Sam, do you have to tell the whole world?"

"I don't think that will be necessary," he teased. "I think you already did." He leaned closer, his voice an octave lower. "These walls are pretty thin, you know."

With a bogus withering look, she crammed the helmet on her head and climbed awkwardly behind him. "I shouldn't even be leaving. The electrician is coming at four, and the roofers—"

Sam looked over his shoulder and rolled his eyes. "God, will you just relax for once? I want you to see

Eden State Park. It's not that far away, and you have to eat lunch, anyway. Why not do it somewhere pleasant?''

She hit him on the shoulder. "I have work to do, and you're not helping."

He grinned lewdly. "I can help with other things. . . ."

"God, you're awful," she said, returning his grin.

"Yeah, and you love it." He reached around and pulled her against him.''Now let's go—hang on."

He put the big motorcycle into gear and swung around the parking lot, Charlotte throwing her arms around his waist, pressing herself against his broad back. As they pulled out onto 98E, she was terrified, excited, and turned on—all in one astonishing moment.

The powerful engine throbbed beneath her, sending up unexpected shock waves, waves that echoed the passion they'd shared last night, and the night before, and the night before. . . . Charlotte tensed, every muscle in her body telling her motorcycle rides were dangerous and foolhardy, impetuous and breathtaking. Her palms were so slippery she could hardly hold on to Sam's shirt, but instinct won her over—just as it had last night and every other night she'd found herself in Sam's arms.

As Sam accelerated, the motorcycle seemed to fly, the highway beneath them turning into a dizzying blur of black, yellow, and white. Charlotte's helmet kept her hair from her eyes, but she could still feel the sting of the sea air on her cheeks as they flashed through the flat landscape of white sand, emerald water, and blue sky. Her stomach turning as fast as their wheels, she clutched Sam to her, his hard back pressing against her breasts, his flat stomach taut beneath her fingers. In a flash, her fear dissolved, and suddenly she felt free and young and sexy. She laughed, throwing her head back against the metal backrest.

Sam turned and looked over his shoulder, grinning as he took her in. "Like it?" he yelled.

"No," she shook her head and cried. "I love it!"

She put work, the bank, the condos—everything out of her head and gave herself up to the sensation of riding the bike. Sam was a skillful driver, maneuvering the heavy Harley through the traffic so smoothly that she relaxed completely.

"You're a good rider," he called back to her, nodding his head. "You've got the rhythm down already."

Charlotte beamed, a mischievous whim bringing out the tease in her. "Of course, I have." She made her eyes grow large and round and pressed herself against him even closer. "We've been practicing quite a bit!"

He laughed, a rich, deep sound that warmed Charlotte even more than the hot Florida sun flashing over her bare arms. Once again, she clasped him closer, and he responded by momentarily placing his hand over hers at his waist before returning his attention to the road.

They wove in and out of the cars and trucks with an easy grace, Charlotte automatically adjusting her seat to the rhythm of the changing gears and the tilting of the massive bike. She pitied the poor, boring drivers in their safe, armored cars; did they know what they were missing?

She glanced over Sam's shoulder, then quickly averted her eyes from the speedometer. She didn't want to know how fast they were going; she only wanted to enjoy. Her glance lit instead on his broad fingers and competent hands as they clasped the heavy bars, easily guiding the cumbersome bike. He drove with as much grace as he made love, taking the huge motorcycle down the highway as adroitly as he'd brought her to climax, time and time again the night before.

Twenty minutes later they were on a small, country lane, the dense foliage on either side producing an air of isolation. Sam slowed and pulled into a gravel covered parking lot. He steadied the cycle while Charlotte climbed off, removing her helmet and staring at the tranquil scene before her. Sam cut the engine, and a thick, dense silence wrapped around them like a heavy blanket.

If she hadn't flown down the highway at seventy miles an hour to get there, she would have thought they'd traveled through time instead of space. Rising before her was the most beautiful old house she'd ever seen. In perfect symmetry, equally spaced columns graced every side, throwing long shadows over the veranda. Tall, gracious oak trees, their limbs heavy with grey moss, surrounded the old house, guarding it from reality.

Afraid to intrude on the serenity of the moment, Charlotte held her breath and stared at the white mansion and its manicured grounds. In front stretched a long reflection pool, the still, green waters covered with lilies. Only the chirping of a million cicadas broke the hushed quiet.

She turned back to Sam, fingers pushing her windblown bangs away from her face. "Thank you for bringing me here," she whispered. "I've never seen anything so gracious, so still. Can you imagine living somewhere like this?"

He stepped closer and slid his fingers into the curve of her jaw and brought her face closer to his. "I'd love to, but since that's not possible, I come here often. It reminds me that I need to stop sometimes, and enjoy what I have. I thought you might feel the same way. What do you think?"

Charlotte's heart had slowed from its previous wild pounding the motorcycle ride had produced, but now Sam's touch sent it racing again. She felt like another woman had climbed inside her skin, had taken over her body to do all the things she'd fantasied about, but had never had the courage to do.

Sam's electric-blue eyes waited for her answer, and

when she smiled, they lit up even more. "I think I love it," she whispered.

His lips brushed over hers in the barest of kisses, immediately making Charlotte wish for more. She reached out, but he caught her hand in his before her fingers reached him. "Do you want to shock the tourists?" he asked, bringing her hand to his mouth.

She flicked her eyes around them. "There aren't any tourists here. We're the only ones." Her stomach tumbled as he placed the tips of her fingers into his mouth and started to suck them greedily. "And, yes, I think I'd like to shock them—right now."

He grinned from around her hand and shook his head. "A few weeks ago, you acted like an old-maid schoolteacher, and now—now, there's no stopping you. What happened? I'm not complaining," he said before she could interrupt. "In fact, I think it's the *real* you, if you want the truth." He placed her hand flat on his chest where she could feel his own heart pounding.

"I . . . I'm afraid you might be right," she answered. "It's like you turned something loose. Something inside of me. I don't really understand, but—"

"But you like it?"

"Yes," she said in wonderment. "I do like it. I like feeling as if I don't have anything to prove, anything to overcome."

He frowned, a tiny web of wrinkles forming near the corners of his bright-blue eyes. "You *don't* have anything to prove—to anyone, and don't ever forget it."

She started to answer, but he cut her off with a devastating kiss. When the shrill cry of a mockingbird brought her back to her senses, Sam was removing a hamper from the back of the cycle. "Come on," he said, holding out a hand, one eyebrow raised. "I brought a great lunch—and a blanket."

"Oh, no," she laughed. "I'm in big trouble."

Holding his broad hand, she followed him down the faint outlines of a long-forgotten drive to the bayou at the foot of the broad lawn. They left everything, including time, behind them.

He opened the hamper and pulled out a plaid blanket, laying it on the ground before her as if it were the finest silk. "Here you are," he said with a wave, "prepare yourself to be wooed."

"There's nothing I'd like better," she answered, sinking to the cover. "Woo away."

From within the basket, Sam removed a plethora of bottles, containers, and bags. Mounds of food and drink quickly surrounded them. "This is incredible," she laughed. "Where in the world did you get all this?"

"I'm very resourceful," he answered. "And besides, don't you know, the way to a woman's heart is through her stomach?"

"I think you're a little confused, Sam. That's the way to a man's heart."

His hands stilled on the container he'd been about to open, and he looked up at her. "How about to yours?" he asked, more serious than she'd ever seen him. "How do I get it?"

In the thick, humid silence, she met his stare. "I think you already have."

His lips curved into a sensual line that reached out and tied her into a tumultuous knot. "That's good, because I'll be needing an extra heart—I think I've lost mine."

He leaned across the blanket and let his lips trail over hers in the softest of kisses, the warmth of his touch making her shiver paradoxically in the bright sunshine. "I need you, Charlotte," he murmured. "I hate like hell to admit it, but I need you. You're like some kind of drug that's in my blood. The more I taste you, the more I want you. I love you, Charlotte."

Her heart lurched, and all she could do was answer his kisses with some of her own, her arms going around his waist, her hands flattening against his muscular back. While the insects hummed and the birds flew overhead, she lost herself in the feel of his hard body and warm caresses. Finally, he lifted his mouth from hers, their eyes locking.

"I love you, Charlotte," he said. "I didn't mean to— I didn't even *want* to—but it happened anyway."

Her throat ached as she stared into his glittering blue eyes. "I love you, too, Sam," she said, her voice breaking with emotion. "What are we going to do about it?"

He pulled her to him, crushing her against his chest, his hand threaded in her hair. "This should be making us happy," he said, "not miserable. Instead, we sound like we've got some kind of disease."

She giggled against his T-shirt, then pulled back to look at him once more. "Myrtle told me being in love was like that."

"It doesn't have to be," he said, pulling her heavy curls away from her neck. "We can make it something special, Charlotte. Stay here—in Destin—and let me prove that to you."

She turned her head toward the lake where a small flock of baby ducks were being strictly herded by the mother duck. "My job is in Denver. There's where my life is."

"Are you sure? You seem to be having a pretty good one, here, too."

"I am, but—"

She broke off, unwilling to say more, but knowing she had to. Sam deserved the truth; he'd given her that and much, much more. "God, I hate to think what my life might have been if I'd married Jonathan."

"You'd be stable."

"Yes."

"You'd be responsible."

"Yes."

"You'd be bored out of your mind."

She laughed out loud, the sound sending the ducks on the water paddling furiously to the other side. "I think you've saved me from that." She tilted her head toward the parking lot. "Motorcycle rides, picnics during the week, wild nights of passion!" She arched her eyebrows, mocking his earlier expression. "You may be a lot of things, but boring is definitely not one of them."

He reached out and took her hand between his. "And am I what you want?"

Her amusement fled at his seriousness, replaced by the confusion she'd been feeling for weeks. "I . . . I love you but there are things I want, goals I have, that I'm not sure fit in with your plans."

"How do you know what I want? You've never asked me."

She looked at him, her heart pounding with nervousness. "I've been too scared. I didn't think you wanted . . ."

"That I never want marriage, a family, a home life?"

"Y . . . yes." Her mouth turned dry with anxiety and her thudding heart revved up another notch.

His gaze didn't waver from hers. "I didn't have those things when I was a child either, Charlotte—just like you. But, we both have choices now. You made one to search for someone you thought could provide you with that. I choose to ignore it. Maybe we should both change. At least, think about meeting in the middle."

She swallowed hard. Sam as a father? Sam as a hard-worker? Somehow the image didn't fit the man beside her, no matter how desperately she wanted to believe that it could.

"I want you to think about it," he said with a look of surprising determination. "In a few weeks, you're going to be finished with the condos, and you'll be talking about leaving. I know how much your career means to you, but sometimes you need to listen to your heart, instead of your mind."

She put her hand up to her throat. "I . . . I can't do that, Sam. I have to think things out, work it through."

"I understand that. But I also think you're due for a change. Think about that, too."

That night, sleep was elusive. She finally gave up and rolled out of bed, padding barefoot to open the glass door leading to her patio. Stepping quietly to the wooden deck, Charlotte plopped down in the plastic chair, her loose white nightgown flapping gently in the soft, ocean breeze.

Hearing the waves lap the shoreline, Charlotte closed her eyes and let the night sensations wash over her. Pungent, warm air. Sea gulls crying. A slight mist covering her skin. The faraway roar of a motorcycle—

Her eyes flew open, and she leaned forward in the chair, staring down the beach, searching for that single headlight. It had to be Sam; nothing but a Harley had that deep-throated rumble. Her eyes hunted through the velvety blackness, but the only lights she saw were in the sky, stars blinking back, silent and distant. The faraway throbbing faded.

Disappointed, she sat back in the chair. She'd told Sam she would think, but she'd lied. Thinking was the *last* thing she wanted to do tonight. She wanted his arms around her, his lips on hers. . . .

She knew she was falling in love, and there was absolutely nothing she could do to stop the free-fall tumble into disaster. Every minute of the day, she pondered the situation, paying less and less attention to the task at hand. When the painter asked her to approve the outside trim color, she stared at the siding until he'd prodded her into an answer. When the electricians put up the wrong ceiling fans in three of the condos, she didn't even notice till Sissy pointed out how awful they looked. And Sam was the one who'd finally told her there was something funny about the rolls of carpet that had been delivered. She'd barely stopped the installers before royal plum, the most awful shade of purple she'd ever laid eyes on, had gone into the first condo.

It had taken her an hour to convince them she hadn't ordered it, and only after the installer's boss had called from the Beach Shack—a lounge down the road that was to be the final home of royal plum—did they really believe her.

To top it off, Jonathan continued to call and check on the progress of the remodeling. Their conversations were always short and to the point, but his voice was more frosty than ever, and Charlotte was doubly glad she'd told him over the phone that their relationship was over. She couldn't imagine what it would be like to be in the same office with him.

When her job here was finished, however, she'd be going back, and that was a source of even greater confusion. All her life she'd devoted herself to her career, and now she was faced with a tremendous choice. The temptation to stay with Sam, to cruise along without thinking of the future, was almost more than she could bear, and for days her defenses had been slipping. Sam had been teasing her, taking advantage of her confusion, too, making it more than clear that he wanted her to stay.

The thought of giving up her job was so foreign, so capricious, that she couldn't even hold on to the consideration for long. Every time the possibility even slipped into her conscious thinking, she'd find herself pushing it away, postponing the inevitable.

She couldn't deny, however, that Sam had shown her a way of life she hadn't even been able to dream of before. He made living more fun, more exciting, more thrilling than she'd thought possible. She *did* have a choice as he'd pointed out.

The repairs on Safe Harbor were just about finished, each unit close to perfect, down to the last towel in the kitchen drawer. All she had left were a few exterior repairs, and then she'd be finished, the project over, her job complete—everything neat and tidy, except her life.

The thought of neat and tidy was suddenly very unappealing. She ran a trembling hand through her dark hair, and bit her lips. Neat and tidy wasn't what she wanted anymore. Sam was what she wanted.

She loved him.

Her hands grasped the edges of the hard patio chair, her knuckles turning white beneath the tan she had acquired. Did she love him enough, though?

Her dark eyes stared out over the moving water, but she didn't see the waves. She saw instead her father—the man she'd never been able to please and would never have the chance to.

Charlotte's hand went to her throat where her pulse began to beat heavily. The two men *were* very different, despite her first thoughts to the contrary. Sam was nothing like her father, and even if he didn't enjoy working that didn't mean he was a bum. Maybe he didn't like to work, and maybe he liked his beer, but that didn't make him an awful person. She was beginning to like the very same things, and nobody worked harder than she did. Usually.

She stood and stretched, reaching for the balcony, her mind in turmoil. As much as she'd like it, nothing would be resolved tonight. She turned to go inside the condo just as the swell of the motorcycle's engine reached her, stopping her steps instantly.

As she watched in amazement, Sam pulled up, right outside her balcony, the heavy wheels of the motorcycle silent as they plowed through the sugary sand. She hadn't seen the headlight because he didn't have it on.

He wore no helmet and only a ragged pair of cut-offs. His bare chest gleamed dully in the silvery shadows and his face was completely obscured. With one slim finger, he motioned for her to come to him. She walked slowly down the steps toward him, her long nightgown dragging in the white sand like a bride's train.

"What are you doing?" she asked, looking at her watch. "It's almost two A.M."

"What are *you* doing?" he asked in return. "I thought you wanted to think."

"That's all I've been doing." Dark circles ringed her eyes and lines of anxiety marred her forehead. Sam instantly wished he could kiss away the confusion that was plaguing her so heavily, even though he knew he was the source of her turmoil.

"Come on," he said gently, tilting his head toward the back of the cycle. "I ride when I need to think. Maybe it'll help you, too."

She grabbed two handfuls of her thin nightgown and held them out from her side. "I'll have to—"

"Don't change," he said, shaking his head. "No one's going to see us anyway—at least, I hope they won't."

"But—"

"Charlotte, it's illegal for me to even be riding on the beach. If anyone sees us, wearing a nightgown's going to be the least of your troubles."

She threw her hands up in a motion of acquiescence, then climbed on the leather seat behind him. "All right," she said in his ear, "but if we both get thrown in jail, who's going to bail us out?"

"Myrtle," he answered with a smile. "She's done it for me before—no problem."

Instead of the frown she would have once directed at him, Charlotte just grinned and slipped her hands around his waist. As he quietly revved the engine and turned the huge motorcycle around, she cuddled closer to him, the thin cotton of her nightgown a nonexistent barrier between his skin and hers. Mentally, he shook his head, his delight over her remarkable changes too great to voice. In the few short months she'd been there, Charlotte Huntington had turned into a woman he could love—and did.

The motorcycle skimmed the water's edge as Sam skillfully maneuvered down the lonely beach. There was nothing between them and civilization, and he took advantage of their solitude, letting the powerful Harley reach its maximum speed.

They traveled on the edge of the world, dipping between reality and the velvet night, the stars as their only guide. Allowing the spray from the foamy waves to cool them, they flew over the boundary of water and sand, danced the ballet between love and desire.

For endless miles, Sam drove. The darkness held no fears for him—only sensations. The warm perfection of Charlotte against his back, the cool touch of the ocean, the forlorn cry of the gulls overhead. Wind rushed through his hair and into his mind, blowing away the complications of life and the complexities of reality, and when he finally slowed, then stopped, he knew Charlotte felt the same way. He could feel it in the easy way she now held her body against him.

They were on a lonely stretch of sand, far from the plush condos, away from the family resorts—totally, absolutely alone. He put down the kickstand and turned, straddling the engine to face her. Like a whispered secret, the darkness wrapped around them.

Ghostly white waves flirted against the motorcycle's wheels, coming near but never touching. Sam leaned toward Charlotte and tightly encased her in his arms as a cloud covered the moon's eyes.

In the darkness, he breathed in her perfume, moving his hands across her back to reach into her tangled hair. His lips found her neck and nibbled, the taste of her like nectar. "I want you, Charlotte. Here, now."

Her eyes met his in a clash of mounting desire, and he saw her swallow hard, her throat moving in the moonlight. Without saying a word, she told him what she wanted, too.

The white cotton nightgown drifted down to the wet sand.

ELEVEN

When the phone rang the next morning at seven o'clock, Charlotte blinked her eyes and shook her head, sleep fogging her mind. Sand scattered over the dark blue sheets like snow. Taking a deep breath, she opened her bleary eyes and snatched up the receiver on the fifth ring.

Jonathan's nasal voice assaulted her. "Well, it's about time. Where were you? Lying on the beach?"

"Hello, Jonathan," she answered wearily. "And how are you this morning?"

"I hope you've finished down there, Charlotte, because I'm pulling your ass out of the fire."

Her cloudy mind instantly cleared at his unexpected vulgarity—it was totally out of character. She blinked rapidly and pushed her hair from her forehead. "Excuse me?"

"I have a client that's flying in to look at that godforsaken property." He pulled in his breath with a sharp sniff. "It wasn't easy, but I managed to talk him into the trip. With any luck at all, you should be able to convince him to buy Safe Harbor. If you can't, you're in big trouble. There's nothing else I can do to correct your mistake."

As always, his stinging words hurt, but this time she spoke out, no longer fearing his censure. "As I recall, Jonathan, the bank backed me on this loan. It might not have been the greatest idea in the world, but I didn't decide all by myself."

"But you promoted it."

"Yes, I did. And you agreed with me—or have you forgotten?"

A significant pause buzzed down the line, then he spoke. "I don't believe that's relevant right now."

"It *is* relevant, damnit. I didn't create this mess all by myself; I had help, yet every time you've called, you've done nothing but criticize. At least I'm here doing something about fixing it, not hiding behind some desk in Denver."

His voice was icy. "*Hiding*? Is that what you think I'm doing?"

"You aren't here helping, that's for sure."

"Someone has to keep business going, Charlotte. *Someone* with half a brain."

She sputtered, her anger reaching such gigantic proportions she could no longer keep it under control. "That's for damn sure—half is all you've got. And I'll be happy to tell you which half got left out. Do you want to know, Jonathan?"

Clutching the phone to her ear, she'd scrambled up from the bed, her breasts heaving with the release of her rage, her words running together with wild abandon. "The half that cares, that's what. The half that can talk decently to other people, the half that gives a damn about something other than money and timetables."

"Charlotte—"

"No, let me finish," she cried, her hair tumbling around her bare shoulders like a dark silk scarf. "For years I put up with your cold-fish attitude, your superiority, your condescending ways. I've worked myself to death trying to be what you wanted, and you've done nothing but give me a hard time." She laughed sharply, the slight edge of control she'd been hanging onto slipping out of her hands. "Too bad we can only break up once."

Like a rubber band stretched to the breaking point, the silence over the line grew longer, then snapped. Jonathan's voice was colder than ever. "Winston Barlow is the potential buyer I'm sending you. I want you to wine him, dine him, do whatever it takes to sell that piece of property to him. If you have any questions, call me later—after you've gotten control of yourself."

The metallic tapping of his pen came over the line, a giveaway clue to his level of anxiety. His next words confirmed it. "When you come back to Denver, we'll discuss our relationship. I think you'll realize what a mistake you made."

Charlotte took a deep breath. "My only mistake was ever thinking I could live with you, Jonathan, and I've taken care of that, thank you very much."

She slammed the receiver into the phone's cradle, her hands trembling with anger, her breath ragged with rage. Over her pounding heart, the sound of Sam's laughter and clapping hands rang out. He tumbled her back into the tangled sheets.

"Quite a performance, Miss Charlotte," he said, his eyes raking her with appreciation. "I'm impressed, quite impressed."

The Fourth of July dawned hot and humid. Before Charlotte could even finish her makeup, it seemed like it'd already slid off her face. With one more quick brush of blush, she gave up and headed out the front door.

Sam caught her as she stepped into her rental car. He wore a new bathing suit; red and blue with white stripes.

A single red star covered one cheek. She thought about the tight muscles lying under that star, and her interest must have been revealed in her eyes; he threw his arm around her and kissed her, stealing her breath. When he raised his face, she had a hard time remembering where she was. "Hey, babe. Where're you going?" he asked. "The party's about to begin."

The event had been planned for weeks. Myrtle had been stockpiling beer for days, Sissy and Margaret had been baking, Paul had been smoking fish. Juan had raked the sand at least half a dozen times, even drawing designs in the powdery white stretches. They'd all done something to help with the party and now she wasn't even going to get to go.

"I've got to go to the airport," Charlotte answered with more anger than she wanted to show. "Jonathan's buyer is coming—remember?"

"Damn!" Sam peeled off the dark sunglasses that were hiding his eyes. "I completely forgot about him. Is that today?"

Distress welled inside of her. "He set it up without asking me. There was nothing I could do about it."

"Oh, I know that—I guess it just didn't register that today was the day."

Her hand went to his face and eased the angry lines from his forehead. "As I recall, you weren't paying attention at the time."

He captured her hand with his, his quick-silver temper disappearing. "Ah, yes," he said. "You distracted me."

Placing her hand on his chest, he wrapped his other arm around her and pulled her closer. "How about distracting an old soldier again?" he grinned. "After all, this *is* a national holiday. Aren't you patriotic?"

She giggled, her own irritation at the task ahead dissolving in the face of Sam's teasing. "Sure, I love my country."

"Come on, then," he said, tilting his head toward his condo. "I'll put on a fireworks display—just for you."

Charlotte's breath caught in her throat as he lowered his head to hers and kissed her. When he pulled back, he stared at her, his blue eyes blazing in the hot summer day. "Interested?"

"Believe me, there's nothing I'd like better, but I'm late already. I have to go pick him up."

Sam dropped his arms and let her step out of his embrace. "He can't take a taxi?"

"Apparently not. Jonathan told me to be there. I guess he wants me to impress him; after all, he is a potential buyer for Safe Harbor."

Sam's jaw tightened. "I really was hoping we could have some time together."

"I know. I'll probably have to take the buyer out tonight, too," she warned.

"You're going to work all day?" His hands knotted into hard fists beside his bare legs as his face darkened under his tan with unfamiliar irritation. "You could have told Jonathan we were having a party. Christ, Charlotte, you knew about this for weeks. I'd think you'd be able to take one day off."

His words whipped at her like stinging ocean spray. "I've taken plenty of time off," she argued. "This is why I'm here, Sam. The whole purpose of my trip was to fix up these condos and find a buyer."

They'd moved to her car, and now he stood beside the door as she climbed inside.

"I know that, but I thought you'd take off the Fourth of July. Most people do."

She started the engine then reached out and took his hand. "I'm sorry, Sam, I really am, but selling these condos *is* the reason I'm here. I couldn't very well tell Jonathan it was inconvenient.''

From the look on Sam's face, Charlotte knew that wasn't what he'd wanted her to say, but he smiled tightly then bent down and kissed her. For once, however, the amusement didn't reach his eyes; they stayed glacial. ''We'll keep the beer cold. Maybe you'll have time later.''

As she drove to the airport, the more Charlotte thought about Sam's words, the angrier she got. He *was* right; most people did take off on the Fourth of July. Why couldn't Jonathan have worked out another date to show the developer Safe Harbor? She hadn't realized it until now, but she'd really been looking forward to the beach party.

Her hands tightened on the steering wheel as she turned into the small airport's parking lot. When she'd arrived in Destin, she'd been satisfied to work fourteen hours a day and holidays, too. She was a different person now, with a tan and a lover to prove it.

She pulled into a parking spot, cut the engine, and rested her head against the wheel. And what was she going to do about it? She was a different person, but was it for the better? What was she going to do when it was time to return to Denver?

For weeks, she'd been denying that reality, but now the project was complete, and she couldn't ignore the situation any longer. She loved Sam, but she loved her career, too. That corner office was a goal she'd been aiming at for years. How could she even think about relinquishing it?

At the sound of an overhead jet, Charlotte raised her eyes to the blue Florida sky. She almost felt guilty at the traitorous thought. Give up her career? And for what? Sam was not into commitments, and that was *exactly* what she had to have.

She sighed, opened the car door, and headed for the

terminal. In a matter of minutes she found the gateway, but her thoughts refused to stay calm. Like a shimmering mirage, the idea of giving it all up, moving to Destin, living with Sam, enjoying the Fourth of July, teased her as she waited for the plane outside the window to stop.

When she saw who got off the jet, her heart stopped. Jonathan!

Charlotte's hand went nervously to her small pearl earrings, and she swallowed hard. She'd never even considered that Jonathan might show up, and a flush of dismay darkened her face.

As he descended the staircase from the plane to the ground, Jonathan stopped and turned to look at the tall, stark man behind him. Charlotte stared, her agitation growing by the minute. Jonathan was bad enough, but the man beside him was even worse. If that was the buyer—and he had to be—they were in real trouble. He reminded Charlotte of a shark she'd seen lying on the beach one afternoon.

A grey suit hung over his spare frame, and one thin hand held down strands of silver hair that were being lifted by the breeze. Dark sunglasses covered his eyes, but the cheeks underneath the tinted lenses were sharp and angular, the lips a slashed line that looked as though it never lifted.

As they entered the small terminal, Jonathan held open the glass door for the older man, then entered behind him. When Jonathan saw Charlotte, he smiled pleasantly and extended his hand. "There you are, Charlotte," he said, taking her fingers into his. "And right on time, I see."

Instantly, Charlotte juxtaposed the man who now held her fingers in a dry grasp and the man who had held her so warmly all night. She found herself yanking her fingers away from Jonathan's grasp and turning to his companion. Ignoring Jonathan's slight frown, she held out her hand.

"You must be Mr. Barlow. I'm Charlotte Huntington."

He nodded and took her hand, squeezing it limply and dropping her fingers almost instantly. "We don't have luggage," he said in the way of a greeting, "so let's don't waste anymore time."

Clenching her jaw, Charlotte smiled, then turned on her heel, not waiting for the two men to follow. If they wanted to be rude, she could be, also. The comparisons she'd just made between Jonathan and Sam were reeling in her mind, and even if she'd wanted to find them, niceties would have been hard to come by.

She led them to the car, then followed Winston Barlow's advice, driving as fast as she dared, filling the silence with empty small talk. They pulled into the parking lot of Safe Harbor within a few short minutes, but it'd felt like hours.

She killed the engine and turned with pride to stare at Jonathan in the backseat. "This is it," she said, waving one hand toward the pristine buildings. "Safe Harbor."

He pulled his lips into a tight smile. "They look decent enough," he conceded.

Decent enough? Charlotte felt her eyes widen in disbelief. She'd taken pictures of the units before she'd started work and had sent them to Jonathan. He knew exactly how much better they looked now, and decent enough didn't begin to cover the changes.

Her chest tightened, but she held back her words. "Let's go inside," she said, opening her car door. "I think you'll be very impressed."

Moving toward the sidewalk, Charlotte began to speak. "As you can see, I've replaced the roof, done extensive landscaping, and painted. The units looked extremely rundown when the bank received them, but in reality, the outside needed cosmetic repairs only. Structurally, they're very sound."

"What about the tenants?"

Charlotte tried to hide her surprise at Barlow's question. He didn't look like the kind of man who would care who rented the apartments.

"At the moment, I'm the only person in the bank's units. They weren't in shape to rent. I have it on very good authority, however, that renting them will not be a problem at all. I've spoken to a real estate agent in town and—"

"Who's in the other ones?"

Charlotte blinked at Barlow's obvious bad manners. Jonathan had told her he was a man of few words, but she hadn't expected them to all be boorish.

She swallowed back her first retort, forcing herself into a politeness she didn't feel he deserved. "The remaining six units are owned by another investor and rented on a long-term basis to individuals."

Jonathan broke in smoothly, his eyes boring into her like twin drills. "Sam Gibson?"

"That's right," she replied, her voice steady. "He lives in one unit and has five very stable tenants in the others. They're permanent residents, retirees." As much to get away from Jonathan's stare as anything, she turned. "Let's go inside, shall we?"

"By all means," Jonathan said. He'd removed a pristine handkerchief and was blotting his forehead with it. "This heat is really something. I can't imagine living here in it."

"You get used to it," she said breezily. Digging her heels into the soft blacktop, Charlotte led them to the first condo and threw open the door. She'd made sure the air conditioners were on full blast, and as they entered the newly renovated units, Charlotte's pride took another leap. They looked perfect—cool, inviting, restful.

The two men walked into the pale turquoise living

room, past the white kitchen and small hallway, to stop before the giant glass door leading to the patio. She expected something—some comment—anything, but they stayed silent. She pointed out the perfect details, but her awkward attempts were the only conversation. By the time they'd reached the third condo, she was seething.

She'd never, ever ask Jonathan his opinion, however. And besides, she thought suddenly, she didn't really give a damn what he thought anyway. Why waste her energy on anger?

She turned to the spotless window at the end of the condo, and spotted Sam, standing in the center of a small group beside the volleyball net. As she watched, he divided them into two separate teams, directing Sissy, Margaret, and Paul to one side and keeping himself, Louise, and Myrtle on the other side. Juan stood beside the net, at least a hundred yards from where Charlotte watched.

Despite the window and distance insulating them, not to mention the sound of the surf, she could hear the little old man blowing on the whistle Sam had just handed him. She grinned as Sam turned around and motioned for Juan to stop. Just as she expected, the old gardener mouthed something back, raised his middle finger, and continued to blast away. With a smirk, Sam shook his head and turned back to the women, putting his broad arms around the shoulders of Louise and Myrtle. They were obviously planning their volleyball strategy.

Along with her amusement, Charlotte felt a stab of resentment. She should have been there, too. As much as anyone else, she'd been looking forward to the party, even baking with Sissy and Margaret. Her pie didn't have the fancy crust theirs did, in fact, the top was a little too brown, but she'd felt honored that the two sisters had invited her to help; the dessert table was their pride and joy. They'd all included her, and now instead of sharing in the fun, she was stuck inside with two people she was disliking more and more.

As the two men reentered the room, Charlotte turned around just in time to catch Jonathan's expression as he raised his face to Barlow's. She didn't like what she saw, but she couldn't quite define it; a flicker of avarice, a glimmer of greed?

In another hour they had toured all the units. Barlow was as silent as ever. Plastering on a fake smile, Charlotte turned to Jonathan with the barest nod to include the other man. "Would you like a quick look at the outside?"

She read the no in Jonathan's eyes, but when Barlow said yes, the younger man nodded his head.

"Excellent idea," he agreed. "Let's do that."

Charlotte led the men outside, uneasy about the inevitable meeting she knew would take place. Sam never held back, in love or in war. Part of her trembled with misgiving, but part of her held her breath like a kid getting onto a roller coaster. This would be an interesting confrontation, she was sure. As they rounded the corner and stood back to look up at the roof, Sam sauntered up.

The volleyball game had obviously finished, but a fine sheen of moisture still slicked Sam's dark skin, running in rivulets down the hardened muscles of his chest. As Sam approached the group, Charlotte's tongue automatically flickered over her lips.

His hair, the part that showed outside the blue bandanna he wore low on his forehead, was wet and curling beneath the rumpled scarf. He still wore his patriotic bathing suit and standing beside the two suited men, Sam's lack of clothing was even more pronounced. As he took off his sunglasses to look down at her, Charlotte's breath caught in her throat. His mesmerizing blue eyes were even bluer outside than they were in his bedroom. She held her breath wondering if he would make some overt move, halfway expecting him to do something outrageous. He didn't, though, and the other half of her was disappointed.

As his firm, full lips lifted, Charlotte remembered her manners and with a pounding heart, she introduced the three men.

Sam shook their hands and replaced his sunglasses, covering his eyes with the dark lenses. She risked a look at Jonathan. His face might have seemed wooden to anyone else, but she'd known him a long time. He couldn't hide the threat he felt from Sam, and she spotted it instantly in the way he straightened his back.

"Don't let us interrupt your party," he said to Sam with a dismissive nod toward the beach.

Sam smiled easily, a self-satisfied expression that rocked Charlotte to her toes. His words answered Jonathan, but he looked at Charlotte. "You aren't stopping anything," he replied. "After you leave, we'll pick up right where we left off."

Charlotte coughed behind her hand, and a warm curl of desire tightened in her stomach before she could gain control of her thoughts. She turned and nodded toward Barlow. "Mr. Barlow is thinking of purchasing the bank's units, Sam." She smiled brightly. "If we've impressed him enough, you two may be neighbors."

Sam's eyes turned to the thin, gray man. "Is that right?" he drawled. "You looking for a new place to call home?"

"Hardly." He stared back at Sam, and Charlotte could see his unwavering expression in the reflection of Sam's glasses. He looked as hard and as brittle as the lenses themselves. "And if I were," he continued, "it wouldn't be here."

Sam nodded his head slowly. "I understand," he said in a measured voice. "You probably wouldn't fit in anyway. You look more like the absentee landlord type. That what you have in mind?''

For a moment, Charlotte didn't think he was going to answer, then finally he spoke, his voice laying a track of vague uneasiness down her back. "This would be an investment for me, Mr. Gibson. Nothing more.''

The air was heavy with tension, and Charlotte held her breath as Sam finally redirected his attention to Jonathan.

"And Jonathan—you're Charlotte's . . . boss?" he said in an insolent voice that really communicated what he thought of the banker before him.

Jonathan's cheeks flushed a deeper shade of red, and the awkwardness of the situation intensified. Charlotte held herself stiff, her breath caught in her throat as she watched Jonathan struggle for an answer. The question seemed a simple one, but all three of them knew better. In another time and place, Charlotte almost would have felt sorry for Jonathan—almost.

"Y . . . yes," he finally stuttered. "I am Charlotte's manager."

Sam grinned, an expression that clearly said, "And I'm her lover." "It's a real pleasure to meet you, Jonathan. Any friend of Charlotte's is a friend of mine." He smiled warmly at her as though they were the only two people on the beach. "We've all come to know—and love her—that's for sure."

Jonathan mumbled something, then pulled on his tie and looked over at Charlotte. "We really must be going, Charlotte. I want to go over some details with you. We'll have dinner, if there's a decent restaurant around here, then Winston and I need to return. The plane is waiting to take us back this evening."

Before Jonathan finished speaking, Barlow turned and started walking toward the front of the units. When he saw the developer moving, Jonathan scurried to catch up. Charlotte flicked her eyes to Sam's.

"I caught all that," she said.

"Good," he said in a sultry voice. "You're going to catch even more—tonight." He pulled down his sunglasses and looked at her over the rims, piercing her with such a steady stare, she found herself squirming. "Think about *that* over your business dinner," he said with an insolence she felt in the pit of her stomach, "and I guarantee you'll have a good appetite—but it won't be for your meal."

Sam was dead right. Charlotte thought of nothing but his steady hands and warm bed during dinner. She did everything in her power to get rid of Jonathan and Barlow as soon as possible, but they insisted on taking much longer than she wanted. It was almost midnight before she was back at the condos. She'd missed the party—and Sam. She knocked on his door, but he was not there. Even Punch didn't bark.

Feeling her need to walk, to clear her brain of Jonathan and Barlow, she went to her condo and slipped into the tiny bathing suit Sam had brought her last week. She still wasn't brave enough to wear it during the day, but it was so late now, no one would be on the beach.

She walked quickly to the shore, her legs flashing into the moonlight with the need to move, to feel the air in her hair, the sand beneath her feet. Fifteen minutes later she turned and headed back. Just as she drew even with one of the double chaise lounges, she saw the flicker of moonlight against skin. Sam was waiting for her.

Without a word, she sat down heavily beside the man and his dog, reaching gratefully for the beer Sam held out. Taking a long swallow, she rested her head against the back of the lounge. The overhead cover of the chair was closed enough to give them privacy, but open enough to let the moonlight trickle in. When she turned her face to look at him in the mercury light, Sam's mouth was inches from hers.

His kiss was a gentle one but when he finished she was trembling.

"Was it rough?" he said in a voice that surprised her.

"Yes," she said. "Barlow was as obnoxious as they come. And Jonathan was so cold I thought it was Christmas instead of the Fourth of July."

Sam leaned back against the lounge, his hand light on her bare thigh. "Looks like that's probably a normal state for him."

"It is." She sighed then glanced over at the tanned man lying beside her. "Barlow is going to tender a bid for the units, Sam. He'll probably get them."

He continued to stare at the dark shore. Above them a sea gull cried as if he'd lost his mate. "What was his offer?"

"I don't know," she replied. "To keep it fair, the bank always uses a sealed bid system. No one knows who'll get the property until all the bids are tendered."

Silence stretched between them. Charlotte wanted to reach out, to pull Sam back from the spot he'd retreated to, but she didn't know how, so she stayed quiet. When he finally spoke, his voice was more serious than she'd ever heard before.

"Do you know who Winston Barlow is, Charlotte?"

His tone seemed curious. "He's a developer—someone Jonathan came up with, that's all I know."

With studied nonchalance, Sam reached back into the cooler at his side and pulled out another beer. When Charlotte shook her head at the proffered can, Sam opened it for himself and drank deeply. In the pale moonlight that washed them, she watched his lips gleam and wished that they were making love instead of talking business. With a shock, she thought about how strange—for her—that desire was.

Sam's voice was quiet. "He makes me really uneasy."

With an unsettled start, she remembered her own impression of the man when she'd first laid eyes on him, but she tamped it down. "I . . . I don't really care for him, either, but I think he'll take good care of the units."

"I don't think he cares about people, Charlotte, their lives, their situations. He only wants what will give him more money, more power."

"Oh, come on, Sam." She shook her head. "Isn't that a little dramatic?"

He whipped his face towards her, his eyes pale in the silver light. "No, damnit, I don't think so." Sitting up, he grabbed her arm. "I care what happens to this place, and I don't think Winston Barlow really does. We'd just be another figure in his portfolio. If the units don't perform—he'd sell them, and God only knows to who." He frowned and two lines pulled his mouth down. "My tenants depend on me, Charlotte. Anybody that hurts them is going to have to answer to me."

"Jonathan knows Barlow, Sam. Believe me, if anyone's particular about people, it's Jonathan. I wouldn't worry if I were you."

With obvious effort, Sam smoothed the wrinkles from his forehead. "I'm not worried—at least not about Jonathan. Why are we even wasting time on this?" He turned on his side to stare at her, sliding his hand along her skin, a touch that she felt deep in the pit of her stomach. "I'd rather be loving you." His fingernails brushed lightly against her skin. "Do you realize how many people would kill to have the kind of life we've got—right here, right now?"

"Yes," she said tightly, "but seeing Jonathan made me think about my job, too. I've got to go back soon."

"Why?"

The word hung between them like a decisive sword. "Because I've worked too hard and too long to give up my career. You've known that from the very beginning."

"And I'm just a summer fling?"

"Of course not," she cried. "I don't have summer flings."

His blue eyes bored into her face before he lifted his hand and flopped down to his back. "Right. I forgot there for a minute just who I was talking to."

Charlotte raised up on the cushion. "I was sent down here to do a job, and I've done it. It's time for me to go back." She pulled her bottom lip in between her teeth and spoke again, her voice almost apologetic. "I have a life in Denver. I'm very tempted to give that up, but I can't . . . not without giving it some serious thought."

"That's your problem, Charlotte. You *think* too damn much. Can't you just *feel* for once?"

"Can't you *think* for once?" Automatically, her voice rose. "I have a job in Denver—a job that means something to me."

He turned to her and pulled her into his arms, silencing her anger with a devastating kiss. "We don't have much time left. Let's put it to good use."

She pressed her hands against his chest, but the movement was useless, and they both knew it. He only tightened his arms and pulled her closer. "If you want to think, then think about this."

His lips outlined the tops of her breasts, pushing aside her swimsuit as though it were a mere annoyance rather than her clothing.

"Sam, we're on the beach . . ."

His teeth scratched over her nipples, and she buried her

hands in his hair with a gasp. "Think about me, baby, and ask yourself—"

"Sam—"

Her protest ended in a gasp as he bent his head to his task once more, biting a little harder. She arched closer to him, moaning into the soft wind, pushing her fingers through his hair as the breeze carried off her protest. His hand went slower, then slipped inside the undersized triangle that was the bottom of her bathing suit. With an accuracy that stole her breath, he found the center of her desire and started a series of slow teasing strokes.

"—Ask yourself at 3 A.M. what's more important—a job or this?"

_____ TWELVE _____

Charlotte felt as though she were splitting in two.

The condos were finished, and she had to return to Denver, but every time she thought about packing, her heart would break open a little further. She couldn't bring herself to even take out her suitcases. Now, as she sat on the porch and watched Sam and Punch play with a frisbee, the phone pulled her away from her painful thoughts.

Jonathan's voice brought them sharply back. Without preamble, he spoke. "You've used up your vacation time, and the condos have been finished for two weeks. Are you coming back?"

The pause down the line cut straight into her heart, but she answered the way she knew she had to. "Yes," she said, tears instantly filling her eyes as she turned toward Sam's carefree laugh. "I'm coming back."

"When? Your accounts are getting out of control; the customers are demanding you and no one else. They understood why you had to be gone at first, but now they're getting angry. Frankly, Charlotte, if you don't return by next week, I'll have to assign your files to someone else."

He paused again, then spoke with thinly disguised relish. "You're jeopardizing your career here, you know that, don't you?"

"Yes," she said heavily. She took a deep breath. "I'll be there next week."

"Good," he said. His voice sounded self-congratulatory, as if he'd just convinced a wealthy customer to make a huge deposit. "By the way, we opened the bids this morning. Barlow got the condos."

Charlotte's heart dropped another notch. "He did?"

"I'd think you'd be grateful."

"I guess I'm glad they sold," she conceded, "but frankly, he gives me the creeps."

"Gives you the creeps? What a juvenile expression, Charlotte. Exactly what are you trying to say?"

She frowned into the receiver, but even Jonathan's discouraging tones couldn't dissuade her. "I just don't feel comfortable around him, but I guess he's a pretty good businessman if he was able to outbid everyone else."

"You don't need to worry about it anymore—just be glad that I found him. He may give you the creeps, but he's also saved your skin, you know." The pause echoed down the line. "If I were you, Charlotte, I'd be thinking about how best to express my appreciation."

"Appreciation?"

"He's gotten you out of the mess you got the bank into, and you have me to thank."

Charlotte's hand tightened around the receiver until her nails were white. "I'll give it some thought," she promised between clenched teeth. "I'm sure I can come up with something."

"Your friend, Gibson, didn't help matters, either."

"He's not part of this discussion. Keep him out of it," she warned.

The sharp sniff on the other end of the line sounded

disapproving, but she didn't care. All she wanted was to get off the phone and run into Sam's arms, the knowledge that she wouldn't be there much longer filling her with depression. "I'll be there by the end of the week," she said. "Order the rest of Barlow's papers, and I'll close the deal then."

"He was in a hurry; we already closed."

She hung up the phone and turned, her eyes downcast, her steps heavy. As if her very thoughts had conjured him, Sam stood before her.

"Did I hear that right?" he asked sharply. "By Friday, you'll be gone?"

She nodded her head miserably. "That was Jonathan on the phone. He said I've used up all my vacation." Her voice caught. "If I want to keep my job, Sam, I've got to go back to Denver."

He took her hand and led her to the couch on the porch as she explained that Barlow had bought the condos. They sat down together, and Charlotte stared through the screen at the green Florida water, her pain welling inside like the waves pounding the shore. A sudden thought intruded.

She raised her face to stare at him. "Sam—why don't you move to Denver? You don't have anything keeping you here."

He shook his head gently. "What about my tenants, Charlotte? With Barlow owning the other half of this place, no telling what's going to happen."

"He'll get good tenants, Sam," she argued. "The condos look great now—they'll sell quickly."

He nodded his head slowly, but she could read the regret in his eyes. "Yeah, they probably will," he admitted.

"What's wrong with that?" she cried. "It'll only make your property value go up."

"That's right, Charlotte. And the taxes, too. You know what that means—"

"Your payments *will* be higher, but—"

"And the rents I collect now don't cover the mortgage. *I'm* making up the difference between the rent I charge and the mortgage I pay. In effect, I'm subsidizing everyone but Paul and Louise. No one knows," his blue eyes turned navy, "and I don't want them to, either," he warned.

She nodded her head, her misery only increasing. "That's why you didn't want to help me fix them up. . . ."

He nodded. "That's partly the reason. I also didn't want you to finish the job too fast. I wanted to get to know you, and the longer you took on the condos, the longer you would be here."

Charlotte swallowed hard and wondered how something that had seemed so simple had suddenly turned into a nightmare. She felt sick.

Sam draped his arm around her. "Let's be logical about this," he said. "That's your usual approach, isn't it?"

Without looking at him, she sniffed and nodded. He continued. "All right. You work for a bank in Denver. Why can't you work for a bank in Florida?"

"I've got a career started there. It takes years to get that kind of position."

"Are you going to die young?"

"I'm not planning on it," she answered, smiling for the first time since they'd sat down.

"Well, then, what's the hurry? You've got plenty of time, and while you're climbing the ladder, you and I could be enjoying life."

She stiffened against him, and Sam knew he'd hit the mark. Her next words confirmed his suspicions.

"Enjoying life shouldn't be my first priority, Sam. Making a living should be."

"Who says?" he asked softly, grabbing her chin with his fingers and turning her face to his. "Is that another one of your rules? Kinda like the one about peeling all the shrimp first, then eating them?''

"There's nothing wrong with rules."

"I agree," he said softly, "unless you depend on them too much."

She cut her eyes to his. "Are you saying that's what I do?"

"No, I'm not saying that at all. I *did* do that, however, and it's not any way to live. You need to be flexible, baby, go with the flow."

This time she didn't smile. "All my life I've made responsible, mature decisions. I don't intend to start living any differently now."

"But you already have, Charlotte," he argued. "Don't you see? It's too late."

As if his touch influenced her too much, she jumped up from the couch and started to pace the tiny porch. "It is not too late, Sam. I may have temporarily misplaced my ambitions when I got here, but believe me, I'm in control of them again. I don't *want* to go back to Denver, but I can't live my life doing what I *want*. There *are* rules, even if people like you make fun of them."

"People like me—or like your father?"

She checked her stride as if she'd suddenly seen a snake. With narrowed eyes, she stared at him. "What's that supposed to mean?"

He deliberately raised his feet to the coffee table and slowly put them on top of its polished surface. He knew he was in for a fight, but it was time Charlotte looked at reality. "When you first came here, you thought I was a lazy, no-good bum, just like your dad. Right?"

Her eyebrows twitched upwards, then she shrugged her shoulders. "I was wrong. I already admitted that."

"Yes, you did," he said, pausing until her eyes returned to his. "But I don't think that you really thought that—I think you're afraid *you* are your daddy, not me."

Her hands curled into tight fists that she planted on her hips. "That's the most ridiculous thing I ever heard of," she said. Heavy lines crisscrossed her forehead. She licked her lips. "I work harder than anyone I know, harder than my father could ever imagine working. Besides that, my career is my life—my God, that's why we started this argument, or have you forgotten?"

"And have *you* forgotten the first conversation we ever had? The one where I asked you why you worked so hard?"

She stared at him and crossed her arms. "What about it?"

"I asked you then why you worked so hard. You said you wanted to be successful, but when I asked you what success was, you couldn't define it. You avoided the point then, and you're avoiding it now." Raising his arms and crossing them behind his head, Sam leaned back into the cushions, trying to present the picture of nonchalance. Inside, however, he felt like he was arguing for his life—and in a way, he was. If he lost Charlotte, his heart would be gone, too.

"W . . . what are you saying?"

"You work like the devil because you think that if you don't, you'll turn into the same kind of bum your dad was. You've spent your entire life trying to prove to the rest of the world that you aren't him, and you've succeeded. You're a beautiful, successful woman who has everything in the world going for her. You couldn't even be like your father if you tried."

Her jaw had tightened into a stubborn line of resistance as he spoke, and now she trembled before him, her anger begging to be released. She was in control, though, just like always—well, maybe not always, he thought instantly. But the bedroom was the only place where she lost it.

"There's nothing worse than an amateur psychologist," she said, her voice breaking. "You're just saying these things because you can't defend your own actions."

"My actions don't need to be defended."

"Right," she bit back. "You're perfectly happy to spend the rest of your life resting on your laurels."

"Yes, and they're pretty good laurels," he countered. "I *was* successful at my career, and now I intend on being successful in my retirement."

"Then let me have that chance, too. You've had your career, you've had your success. Now it's my time for that."

"But you can have that here."

Her voice rose another octave. "I've got it in Denver. Why look for it here?" She planted her hands on her hips and stared at him. "You move."

The tension flowed across the room like hot lava, but Sam refused to budge. He dropped his arms to his chest and crossed them.

"No."

"You're being unreasonable."

"So are you."

She threw her head back and stared at the ceiling, her throat cording with anger before she turned back to him. "I've got to take my turn, Sam. Try and see that. You had yours, now I've got to have mine."

He shook his head, dropping his hands to his knees and leaning forward. "If you wanted it for yourself, I'd understand, but our situations are totally different. My success was for myself—yours is for someone else. Someone who never gave a damn to begin with."

He stood up and moved closer to her, hating the pain that now darkened her grey eyes to slate. "I don't know what demons plagued your father, Charlotte, but they've become his legacy to you—a legacy you don't have to accept. Throw off the past, for God's sake, and live life in the present—with me."

She dropped her eyes and wet tears trailed down her cheeks. Sam wanted to wipe them away, but he knew that if he touched her, he'd never let her go, and this had to be *her* decision.

"I can't just leave my job," she said brokenly. "It's all I've had for years. Until I met you, it was my entire life." She looked up at him, the pleading shadows behind her eyes almost killing him. "Please understand, Sam. I have to go back."

In a month, her tan had faded under the pale Denver sky.

In a million years, her feelings for Sam would. They had to.

Every day she went to her office, in control and focused. Tasks were accomplished, goals achieved, and for at least ten hours a day, she was able to put Sam from her mind.

At the most awkward times, however, a memory would creep into her mind and steal her composure. She'd pick up a letter, but her eyes would go to the window instead of the missive in her hand, and the cool mountains would make her long for a different sight. Suddenly, she'd see the movement of water, the cry of gulls, the frantic activity that marked the Destin beach, and her heart would turn erratic.

Sometimes she'd be in the middle of dinner, soup spoon halfway to her mouth when she'd stop, her thoughts spiraling instantly to a hot beach and cold shrimp, the reality of her lonely apartment fading out of sight.

She knew her heart was gone, and sometimes she thought she'd lost her mind, too.

Had Sam been right?

If what he'd said was the truth—if she'd lived her life for a father who didn't even care, couldn't care—then everything she'd done had been for nothing. Her accomplishments meant little, her successes less.

Today, for the hundredth time, she looked around her office, the trappings of her life visible in every corner. Awards for service, diplomas, recommendations—everything she'd worked so hard for suddenly seemed pointless. It really didn't matter who she'd done it for—none of it was worth giving up her life for. Was it?

Her hands tightened against her arm chair, the smooth leather cool to the touch. She *did* love Sam, with all her heart. He made her feel alive and wonderful and young and sexy. All the great emotions she'd never experienced before, Sam had brought to the surface. There wasn't a man alive who could make her heart sing, her passion soar, her pulse race like Sam Gibson could.

Her eyes flickered back over her desk. Had she been wrong for ten years? Had she devoted her life to something that wasn't worthwhile?

She dropped her head into her hands and sighed. Her career had been her lover, her home, her life, and she might have been unhappy, but she'd been productive. Nothing could take that away from her.

Turning to the stack of folders on the edge of her desk, Charlotte opened the first one and went back to work.

The days passed in a painful blur, and Charlotte continued to work, often as much as twelve hours a day. She did busy work, she did important work, she even did unnecessary work. But her heart continued to bleed even as her brain was occupied. Somehow, through the heart-breaking fog, though, her mind was taking in facts and assembling details. She still wasn't prepared, however, when the final picture fell into place.

Jonathan's office was as pristine as ever, she noted, as she waited for him that morning, the carpet freshly vacuumed, the blinds arranged just so. His desk gleamed, the marble completely empty of clutter with only his Mont Blanc pen and a pad of yellow paper marking time. As she moved toward his window, the coldness of the decor struck her. The room was devoid of any personality except for the Chamber of Commerce awards, Better Business Bureau plaques, and certificates of achievement that lined the wall behind the sofa. His office was as empty as her life.

She sat down abruptly in the closest chair—the one behind his desk. Was *this* what she was working toward? A corner office, but one that bore no testimony to a life outside its confines?

Lost in thought, she didn't hear the door open, didn't even know she was no longer alone until Jonathan spoke.

"Trying it out for size, my dear?"

She stood abruptly. "I . . . I hope not."

He frowned as he came around the edge of his desk, his heavy aftershave reaching her before he did. Once she'd liked the fragrance, but now, it seemed overblown and counterfeit. As he reached her side, he placed his fingers lightly on her arm.

She glanced down at the hand extending from the white, starched shirt. His silk tie shimmered in the morning light, his polished nails buffed and spotless. For a second, she saw broad, tanned fingers, rough with calluses and dusted with light blond hair. Remembering the peaks they could take her to, Charlotte closed her eyes and swayed momentarily, a wave of desire washing over her. When she opened her eyes, however, it was Jonathan who beamed and moved past her to sit down in his leather chair.

Folding his hands and rocking back in his chair, he smiled as broadly as she'd ever seen him smile. He looked remarkably pleased, and his next words confirmed her estimation.

"The bank is very happy with the work you did in Florida, Charlotte. Of course, if Barlow hadn't purchased the condos, I don't mind telling you, things would be very different."

She rested her hip on the edge of the credenza and stared at him. "Really?" she said. "You mean if they hadn't sold—if *you* hadn't found me a buyer—my work would all have been for naught?"

He frowned lightly. "No, not exactly, but the situation would be very different."

I'll bet, she thought silently, looking down at him, the work she'd done fresh in her mind. She lifted her hand and stared at her nails, trying to act casual. "Tell me something, Jonathan. How did you find Winston Barlow? It seems so fortuitous."

Obviously pleased by her praise, he simpered. "No, my dear, chance had nothing to do with it. I applied myself diligently to finding a buyer." He lowered his face and stared up at her, as though he were looking over the reading glasses he sometimes wore. "Let's face it, I was trying to save your sweet little ass."

Charlotte pulled in her breath sharply. Thoughts ran through her head, and she realized with a start that he was acting very strange. What was going on? She hid her suspicions behind a mask of indifference. "And save it, you did, Jonathan. That doesn't satisfy my curiosity, however."

He shrugged and glanced out the window. "Barlow and my older brother went to school together. Actually, we go back a long way—our families and theirs, that is. When I heard that the condos would be available, I called him. He's a big investor, and I thought he'd be interested."

"And, naturally, he was."

"Yes. It's not a bad little property, actually."

She drew a line in the plush carpet with the toe of her high heel. "That's true. The people who live there really seem to like it."

"That might change," Jonathan chuckled.

Charlotte's stomach knotted. "W . . . what do you mean?"

Jonathan's face flushed slightly, and he cleared his throat as if he wished he could take back his words. "All I meant is that Barlow's a very astute businessman, Charlotte. If those tenants have been happy with the way Sam Gibson was managing things, I'm sure they'll be even more satisfied with Barlow's management team." Regaining his composure, he grinned, a cocky smirk that made her stomach crawl. "Sam won't be there for long. Barlow will tender him an excellent offer just to get him out of there, then he'll own the entire project."

Charlotte shook her head. "Never. Sam wouldn't sell those condos if his life depended on it."

Jonathan steepled his fingers and looked at her over their manicured points. "Don't be a ninny, Charlotte. Anyone will sell something if they can make a profit."

Not Sam! As the thought shot into her brain, Charlotte was forced, once more, to compare the man before her and the man she'd left behind. *Jonathan* might do anything for a profit, but Sam? Never. To Jonathan, money meant everything, and suddenly the pieces she'd seen all week fell into the right places.

Barlow hadn't just lucked into the low bid—Jonathan had looked at the other bids and told Barlow what price would get him the units!

Hiding her suspicions was the hardest thing Charlotte had ever done, but she knew she'd have to be calm if she wanted Jonathan to tell her the truth. She raised her eyes to him. "I saw Barlow's bid for the condos in the file."

With a smooth aplomb, Jonathan nodded. "The vice president of loans will be handling the situation from now on. It's out of your hands."

"Fine," she said calmly. "But maybe you can teach me something. Tell me how Barlow's bid got so close to the nearest offer?"

"Amazing, wasn't it?" Jonathan answered easily. "I thought that was remarkable, also." He shook his head, leaning back into the chair. "I guess that's what happens when you've been in the business world as long as he has. He can cut closer to the quick than the rest of us."

Charlotte felt her stomach tighten. She was getting nowhere; she might as well be blunt. "Did you tell Barlow what the bids were, Jonathan?"

His voice was frozen, and so was his expression. "Why would I do that?"

"My first guess would be money. How much did he pay you, Jonathan?"

Jonathan let the chair fall forward, his face a mask of indignation. When he spoke, his tone was harsh. "Are you implying I acted less than ethically, Charlotte?"

"Did you tell Barlow what the bids were?"

His knuckles turned white against the arms of the chair. "That would be highly dishonest, not to mention illegal. Surely, you read the ads we placed in the local Florida papers as well. Anyone could bid on those condos. It was simply shrewdness on Barlow's part that he won them."

"Shrewdness or help from you?"

"I've had enough of this nonsense," he said in a suddenly cold and relentless voice. "I've done everything I could to help you out, and for thanks, you're questioning my ethics. I thought you might have learned something from this entire situation, Charlotte, but instead, you've come back a different woman." He shook his head angrily, a long lock of brown hair falling over his forehead. With unsteady fingers, he pushed it back into place. "Is this what Sam Gibson taught you?"

Hearing Sam's name coming from those dry, cruel lips was more than Charlotte could bear. She jumped up. "No," she blazed. "Sam taught me something much more valuable—how real people live, and love."

All the color drained from Jonathan's flushed face, and for two seconds, Charlotte almost felt sorry for him. His next words destroyed that feeling, and the last bit of respect she had for him. "You witch," he said with soft rage. "I was prepared to share everything with you, including the money. I can't believe I was so naive. I should have known better."

Her defense was automatic, the words falling out with reckless disregard for her previous feelings. "Known better?"

"Bad blood, Charlotte. I've known all along about your father but I kept it to myself. I thought you'd overcome your natural bad tendencies. I see now that I was wrong."

Once his words would have cut her to the quick, but now a surge of awareness washed over Charlotte that empowered her with understanding and courage. Her voice was strong, and she looked him right in the eye. "For once, we agree, Jonathan. You *were* wrong, but you don't understand yet exactly *how* wrong."

Charlotte sat on the bench outside the board room and tried to dry her hands unobtrusively against her skirt. She'd had the floor for over two hours, and they'd been the worst two hours of her life.

In her mind's eye, she saw the ten men and four women

as they'd listened to her explanation and viewed her evidence. At first, it'd been clear they didn't believe her. She was risking her job, but the truth had to be told. The more she showed them, the more she'd sensed a subtle shift in their attitudes. There was no way Barlow could have gotten so close to the lowest bid without inside help. The obvious culprit was Jonathan.

He had denied the charges, of course, and Jonathan had sounded convincing, she had to admit. Despite the glowering looks he'd directed toward her, he'd looked very persuasive in his Brooks Brothers suit and old school tie. Good looks wouldn't win over evidence, however, and Charlotte knew she'd presented a solid case. The bank would be rocked by a scandal like this, and she knew the fourteen people behind those doors would be giving that possibility all the consideration it deserved. In this day and age, banks were pretty shaky to begin with; bad publicity like this only shook their foundations more.

Restlessly, she stood up, glancing at her watch. The doors had been closed for more than an hour; it seemed like years.

She stepped toward the service bar situated beside the window, reaching for a cup as she looked down. Thick glass insulated her from the street sounds far below, but like a magnet, her eyes were pulled toward the traffic. Her heart stopped.

Twenty stories beneath her a man on a black motorcycle waited at a red light. He wore dark jeans and a battered jacket. As she watched, his hands tightened on the handlebars then twisted. The mechanical thunder rumbled deep in the pit of her stomach, and Charlotte's mouth went dry. For one quick heartbeat—*Is it? No, it can't be*—she let her hopes flare, then reality snuffed them out. Sam was thousands of miles away, and even if he wasn't, if by some sweet miracle that *was* him on the street, he'd come no nearer.

As the light changed and the biker took off, Charlotte closed her eyes and leaned her head against the cool glass, allowing, for once, the quick, hot sting of tears to form behind her lids. She missed Sam like she would miss her heart had it been ripped from her body.

The door to the conference room opened behind her, and she straightened instantly, dusting her hand across her cheeks before turning. Jonathan stepped into the waiting room, his frozen smile turning downward as he closed the door and saw her.

"Well," he sneered, "if it isn't Miss Goody Two-Shoes." He adjusted his tie and stared at her, disgust darkening his brown eyes. She'd once thought of them as warm, but now they were like two pieces of glittering topaz. "Your lies will never convince them, Charlotte."

"They weren't lies," she said wearily, stepping away from the coffee service, trying to keep the cup in her hand from trembling. "Everything I said in there was the truth, and you know it."

"I know one thing," he said, moving toward the silver service and pouring his own brew with steady hands. "When they open those doors and call us back in there, you're going to be finished." He brought his cup up to his thin lips and looked at her over the rim before sipping from it. "You're going to be back where you started—nowhere."

Charlotte told herself his hateful words were spite and nothing more, but they instantly conjured up images from her childhood. Jonathan's face wavered, replaced in her mind with the broad outline of her father's likeness. She shook her head, forcing the ghost to disappear.

Her back straightened again, and she focused on Jona-

"You're mistaken, Jonathan. You're the one that's going to be out of luck—and out of a job."

"Hmmph," he sniffed. "I wouldn't start moving into my office, if I were you, Charlotte."

"I don't want your office," she answered instantly, surprising herself as much as him. "I don't want your office, your job—" she flung out her hand, "any of this."

He stared at her, his eyebrows arching into two perfect curves above his eyes, but just as he opened his mouth to speak, the doors behind them opened. The blank-faced secretary looked directly at them and spoke. "You may come in now. The Board has reached its decision."

THIRTEEN

The tower of boxes moving across the parking lot toward him had two arms and two legs, and for just a moment, Sam's eyes registered the sight, but his brain refused to accept it. Gradually, he realized there was a person behind the traveling pillar—Myrtle. Dropping his own bag of groceries, he rushed forward to help her.

"What in the hell are you doing, Myrtle?" he said, taking the topmost boxes and setting them on the ground. "You're about to break your fool neck carrying all this stuff around."

She muttered something from behind the two boxes she still carried and from around the cigarette hanging at one corner of her mouth, but he couldn't understand her. Tilting her head to the other end of the complex, she repeated her answer. It sounded something like "Mooing."

His ignorance must have been obvious because she finally set her boxes down and pulled the cigarette from her mouth, a cloud of smoke coming with it. "I'm helping a friend move in, you big galoot."

Disbelief knit his eyebrows together, and he stared at

211

212 / CAY DAVID

her, words escaping him. "Move in?" he repeated dumbly. "But I don't have any empty units. Where's your friend moving *in* to?"

Grinning, she stuck one hand on her hip and brought the other one to her mouth to pull deeply on her lipstick-smeared cigarette. "You must be getting old. You've obviously forgotten that you don't own *all* these units anymore." She nodded toward the bank's end of the project. "One of my lady friends that I play bingo with was looking for a new place to roost. When I told her about the bank's units, she got all interested and talked to the real estate lady." Myrtle took a deep hit on the cigarette. "If you ask me, she got a damn good deal."

Sam looked over his shoulder toward the parking lot, then back to the tiny woman in front of him. "They're renting already?"

Her lips squeezed the cigarette until the white paper puckered. "Yup, and very reasonably, I might add." She crammed both fists against her nonexistent hips, the glowing ash of her cigarette flirting dangerously close to her billowing housedress. "I don't mind telling you, I was mighty tempted."

Sam blinked and looked down at the tiny, gray haired woman. "Tempted? What do you mean?"

She rammed the cigarette back between her lips and picked up her boxes. "Follow me," she said. "I'll show ya." She took off down the sidewalk, her purple house slippers raising small clouds of sand with each step.

He trailed behind her until she stopped at the freshly painted door of the last condo and looked up at him expectantly. "Well? You gonna open the door or stand there with your thumb up your—"

"All right, all right," he answered testily. "Just a minute."

"Will you please open the damn door? I ain't as young as you are and my arms are gettin' tired."

Sam reached out and twisted the shiny brass knob. Silently the door glided open, sending out the scent of fresh paint and new carpet as Myrtle stepped in, going immediately to the kitchen and dropping the two boxes she'd been carrying. With a suspicious rattle and thump, they quivered into stillness on the polished linoleum floor.

Looking around, Sam set his boxes down on top of hers. To his surprise, he saw at least a dozen other boxes decorating the empty den and hallway. A frizzed redhead rose up from the center of the confusion, a long cigarette dangling from puckered lips. Black capri pants and a faded crop top told Sam her fashion clock had stopped somewhere about 1954, but the rest had kept on ticking. She was at least eighty.

"Well, hello there! And who are you?"

Myrtle proudly introduced Sam to Maggie, her bingo buddy, and after a few minutes she returned to her unpacking.

"Look around you, Sam." Myrtle picked up the package of cigarettes off the counter, lit one, then moved closer to him, her face wrinkling up in concern. "These units are gorgeous. They're bright, and clean, and pretty. It'd be a dream to live in a place like this."

He covered his hurt with gruff words that had nothing to do with what she was saying. "I thought you liked living next to me."

She narrowed her eyes. "I do, that's why I'm bringing Maggie's boxes in here instead of mine, but look around." She waved her cigarette in the air, indicating the freshly remodeled home. "This is wonderful *and* the toilets work." She breathed deeply then coughed several times. "It even smells good."

"It won't for long with the two of you!" He glanced

toward Maggie's corner of the room. Like a mushroom cloud, a pall of smoke already hung over her.

Silently, Myrtle took another drag, her eyes narrowing, never leaving Sam's face. "But it's nice now, and that's what counts," she said stubbornly.

Suddenly, Sam was tired of hearing what he knew was the truth. He dropped onto one of the bar stools, his fingers resentfully gliding over the smooth, beautiful upholstery. "You're right," he said, his voice exhausted with the effort.

She took one more look at him, pulled on the cigarette, then nodded her head. "You're damned right, I'm right. People need more than beautiful sunsets and cold beer." She leaned against the kitchen counter and tapped the microwave with one hand, a trail of ashes following her movements. "They want fancy ovens, and tile floors, and—"

"Toilets that work," he supplied.

"Yes." She ground the cigarette into the pristine sink, then searched her pockets, coming up with another one and her lighter. Over the flame, she stared at him, then spoke. "You've been acting like a giraffe with a sore throat ever since Charlotte went back to Denver. You aren't mad because I'm telling you the truth, Sam. You understand all that—you're mad at her."

"Did you go to night school to get that psychology degree or was it a mail order item?"

She grinned at him and shook her head. "You aren't goin' to rile me, Sam, so forget it. I can recognize a lovesick man when I see one."

He ran his hand over the smooth formica and avoided her eyes. "Charlotte Huntington has nothing to do with this. I'm sick and tired of hearing about how great these apartments are—that's all." He looked around once more.

"I guess I'm going to have to do something about it, right?"

"You're damned right, but you're crazier than Juan if you believe that's what has you riled!" Like a tiny sparrow's claw, Myrtle's liver-spotted hand clutched his arm. "Admit it, Sam. You're missing Charlotte."

He raised his head to protest, but she held up her hand to cut him off. "Don't lie to me."

Sam stared down at Myrtle, but the admission stuck in his throat. If he voiced it, Charlotte's absence would seem even more permanent.

The silence grew. Behind them, Sam could hear Maggie singing a song. The words were garbled, but it sounded something like 'That Charlie Brown, Oh, he's a clown.' The corner of Sam's mouth twitched up. He looked at Myrtle. "What would you suggest I do first? Paint or work on the plumbing?"

A look of sheer frustration lined her already wrinkled face as she threw her hands into the air, her bony shoulders moving under the red and green housedress. "Haven't you listened to a word I've said?"

He swallowed hard, then stood up, pushing the bar stool out from under him. Myrtle was right, but saying the words then doing something about it were two different things. He interrupted her abruptly. "This new landlord . . . Barlow, whatever, is he around? Have you seen him?"

Myrtle stared at him, then bent over and suddenly started digging in a box by her feet, the ashes from her cigarette falling harmlessly into the cardboard container. If he wasn't going to pay attention to her, then she obviously wasn't going to pay any to him.

"Myrtle?" he raised his voice to be heard over the noise. "Where is he?" he repeated.

Purposely ignoring him, Myrtle continued to remove

battered pots and baking pans from the box at her feet. Finally, she stood up and dropped a large copper skillet, taking her burning cigarette from her mouth and waving it like a pointer toward the unpacked contents. "You're botherin' me, Sam. Can't you see I'm helping Maggie?"

"Who—"

"Try down on the beach." She crammed the cigarette back into her mouth and tilted her head toward a brightly colored umbrella twenty feet outside her patio door. "Might be out there."

His irritation took another giant leap. "On the beach? What in the hell is a landlord doing on the beach? He ought to be up here, seeing if his tenants need any help."

Like a jack in the box, Myrtle stood up, curled her upper lip and put her hands on her hips, the cigarette dangling dangerously from the edge of her mouth. "We don't need any help—in fact, I wish you'd get the hell out of here and let us finish unpacking."

"All right, all right." Sam threw his hands up in disgust and moved toward the patio door. "I'll be back after I talk with this joker. I'll carry the rest of those boxes for you then."

"Don't stay too long," she shot back. "I ain't got all day, you know."

She was lying on her back in the sand, the pink towel she'd carelessly thrown down barely long enough for her outstretched body. At one end, from under a large straw hat, dark hair fanned out over the white powder. Behind tinted glasses, her eyes were shut. At the other end, coral-tipped toes curled slightly. In between, her tiny, blue bikini barely covered her tanned and oiled body. That was okay. What he could see brought back memories of what he couldn't.

Sam Gibson stared at Charlotte Huntington and swallowed hard, his heart beating a reggae rhythm that rivaled the music coming from the teenager's radio blaring from just over the next dune.

What in the hell was she doing here?

His eyes traveled over her bronzed body, taking in the pristine white poodle sharing the shade of Charlotte's umbrella. The dog was sitting up perfectly straight and staring at the waves as if it wasn't too sure of what it was supposed to be doing.

As if taking its measure, Punch circled the elegant canine once, barked, then took off down the beach. With a quick look of apology toward Charlotte, the poodle followed, nipping at Punch's heels as she caught up with him.

At the sound of the yelping dog, Charlotte's eyes flew open, then grew even larger as she turned toward the man blocking her sun. "Hello, Sam," she said evenly. "How are you?"

His heart flipped over inside his chest as her calm grey eyes met his. How had he ever let her leave?

"I'm fine," he lied. "How about you?"

She smiled and nodded once. "Not too bad considering everything."

"Can I sit down?"

She shrugged. "Sure."

Swallowing hard, Sam sank to the sand beside her. He felt like a thirteen year old approaching his first real kiss.

"Wine cooler?" She held out a slick can from the chest behind her.

He took it gratefully, grinning all the while. "Still haven't developed a taste for beer?"

She stared at him straight on, her eyes locking with his like a drowning man holding onto a life line. "No, but I have developed a hunger for a few other things, though."

The humid air made it difficult for Sam to breath. "Like what?" he finally managed.

"Like you," she said.

She spoke so softly he wasn't sure he'd heard right. "I missed you," she continued, her eyes bright behind the tinted glasses.

"What about Denver—the bank, your career?"

She turned her head and looked out over the water, but Sam knew she wasn't seeing the rolling waves. "I found out that things aren't always what they seem," she said, turning back to face him. "You told me I didn't know what success was, but I didn't believe you. Remember?"

Sam wanted to reach out, to take her into his arms, but he was afraid to break the fragile moment. "And now you do?"

She smiled gently. "No. I still don't, but I know now what it *isn't.*" She paused then explained what had happened at the bank.

"You mean Jonathan told Barlow what to bid?"

"That's right. He came in with a bid just a few dollars over the highest bid, so he would have gotten the condos at a ridiculous price. Luckily, the board put a stop to it."

He slapped his knee. "I *knew* that Barlow was—"

She stopped him with a wave of her hand and finished the story. "The bank offered me Jonathan's position," she ended.

He held his breath. "That's what you always wanted, wasn't it? That big corner office?"

"I thought it was until I got it, then I realized that wasn't what I wanted at all. It didn't feel right—in fact, it was as bad a fit as Jonathan's engagement ring had been." She shrugged her shoulders then grinned. "I turned it down, left the bank, and bought the condos when the bidding started over. I'm your new co-owner."

His mouth dropped open another notch. "*You're* the new landlord?"

"Yep," she laughed. "We're partners."

Sam fell into the sand and starting laughing, holding his sides as the joke finally sunk in. "I . . . I can't believe it," he finally gasped. "I'm finally ready to fix up my side, and I've got you for a partner?" He pointed to the cooler and the frolicking poodle that was leading Punch on a merry chase. "You? Lying out here in the sand doing nothing?"

She grinned in return. "I kinda like it."

"I'm sure you do," he said. "But I want to go to work. I can't postpone it any longer. If I do, I think I'm going to have a revolution on my hands."

"Myrtle?"

"How'd you know?"

"She told me when she brought Maggie over to meet me." Charlotte pulled down her glasses and looked at Sam from over the rim. "How will you finance the repairs?"

Sam's grin faded as his hand reached out and tucked a windblown curl behind her ear, then lingered for a moment longer against her jaw. "What would you say to a merger?"

Her eyes lit up. "I think that's a terrific idea. We could refinance the entire project, then use the funds to repair your side. With interest rates—"

"Whoa, Charlotte—" He put one finger over her mouth. "That's a great idea, but not exactly what I was talking about."

She grinned, her face lighting up with love as she reached out and put her palm on his cheek. "I'm kidding, sweetheart. I knew what you meant."

Her touch radiated up his arm and into his heart. "Is that a yes?"

"You bet—but on one condition."

He raised his eyebrows. "You name it."

"I want you to help me live day by day. To enjoy life,

to listen to my heart instead of my head. I may be a lot of trouble, but . . .''

His heart constricted into a tiny ball of tension, then released with a pounding he could hear even over the roar of the emerald waves. "There's nothing I'd like better,'' he said, love deepening his voice as he took her into his arms and pressed her down into the sand. "Trouble like you, I can handle.''